## *"Hello, Jake."*

She never would've imagined herself begging this man for a job. But with her baby's welfare at stake, Rachel's pride didn't matter. Not one iota.

"I'm sorry if I woke you," she said, "and I know I'm probably the last person you want to see…but I'd like to talk to you. It's important."

"Important to who?" He stood in the doorway, bare chested, one hand on the door and the other on the frame, a barrier to keep her out. She could feel his animosity.

At any other time she'd have turned and walked away. Instead, she girded her resolve. If she could just get him to listen…

"To both of us."

Dear Reader,

Welcome to the TEXAS HOLD 'EM continuity series, featuring five poker-playing cowboys from River Bluff, Texas. It was a pleasure to work with the talented authors behind the series: Tara Taylor Quinn, Debra Salonen, Cynthia Thomason and Linda Warren. While the story in *Going for Broke* stands alone, I hope you have the opportunity to get to know all the men who make the small town of River Bluff come to life.

I've always been a cowboy fan and I love the interaction and camaraderie of the men in this series. But *Going for Broke* is more than a cowboy buddy story. It's a story of love, redemption and forgiveness – on several levels.

Jake Chandler and Rachel Diamonte, the woman he falls in love with, have complicated pasts. For fifteen years Rachel has been living with a lie – one that changed the course of Jake's life.

While Jake escaped the town that branded him bad and has since forged a successful life for himself, Rachel chose to marry a man she thought could make her forget what she'd done. But Rachel's marriage dissolved and, with a handicapped daughter to support, she's forced to return to River Bluff. Jake has come back to bury his uncle, and that's it.

But soon Jake and Rachel are facing the biggest challenge of all. Love. Is it possible to love someone who's betrayed you? To forgive? I wasn't sure it was until I wrote "The End." Jake and Rachel need to "go for broke" if they want a future together. I hope you enjoy reading their story.

I always love to hear from my readers. Please come and visit my website at www.LindaStyle.com or write to me at PO Box 2292, Mesa, AZ 85214, USA.

May all your happily-ever-after dreams come true.

*Linda Style*

# Going for Broke
# LINDA STYLE

MILLS & BOON
*Pure reading pleasure*™

*First published in Great Britain 2009
by Harlequin Mills & Boon Limited,
Eton House, 18-24 Paradise Road, Richmond, Surrey TW9 1SR*

© Linda Fensand Style 2007

*ISBN: 978 0 263 87353 5*

38-0109

*Harlequin Mills & Boon policy is to use papers that are
natural, renewable and recyclable products and made from
wood grown in sustainable forests. The logging and
manufacturing processes conform to the legal environmental
regulations of the country of origin.*

*Printed and bound in Spain
by Litografia Rosés S.A., Barcelona*

## ABOUT THE AUTHOR

Winner of the Daphne du Maurier and Orange Rose Awards for best long contemporary romance, Linda Style always dreamed of becoming a novelist, but it took a few years and several detours along the way before that dream came true. A graduate of the University of Minnesota in behavioural science and the Walter Cronkite School of Journalism at Arizona State University, Linda has worked as a case manager, a human rights advocate, a freelance journalist, photographer, management consultant and as the director of the Office of Grievance and Appeals for the Seriously Mentally Ill for the State of Arizona. She began to write full-time in 1998.

To my poker-playing TEXAS HOLD 'EM
buddies – Judy Bowden, Connie Flynn, Laurie
Schnebly, Sharon Swearengen,
Sharyn Liboratore, Peggy Miller and our newest
member, Rhonda Woodward.
Classy ladies – one and all.
You've made researching a lot more fun!

ACKNOWLEDGEMENT
Many thanks to those who contributed to
the research in this story: The San Antonio
Chamber of Commerce, The Bandera Chamber
of Commerce, The National Association for
Down Syndrome. Since this is a work of fiction,
I've taken liberties where necessary.
Any errors are solely mine.

# CHAPTER ONE

"DID YOU REALLY kill the horses?"

The kid gawking at him wasn't more than five years old.

Standing on the left bank of the Medina River, Jake stuffed his hands in the pockets of his leather jacket, his stomach churning like the river below. Fifteen years later, the accusation was still alive.

"My gramma says you burned the barn and the horses died." The boy's eyes sparkled, his excitement over the idea chilling.

"Get back here, Peter." The middle-aged woman grabbed the boy's arm and yanked him to her side. "He'll get mad and then you'll be sorry."

The child made a face as he squeezed

himself between the woman's big legs and clutched the fabric of her baggy pants in his fist.

She turned, then snatched up their fishing gear. "C'mon, Peter. We're not staying here any longer."

"But we didn't catch any fish yet."

Ignoring the boy's protests, the woman dragged him up the riverbank to the road, hustled him into her car and drove away.

A sharp winter gust whipped at Jake's hair, but it felt like a Santa Ana wind compared to the subzero look the woman had given him.

Fire-starter. Barn-burner.

He'd heard the whispers behind his back from the moment he'd climbed off his Harley four weeks ago. He'd come back to River Bluff, Texas, for his uncle's funeral and, even then, even at the graveside service, he'd heard the low whispers.

*Barn-burner.* Bastard son of the town whore.

True or not, that's who Jake Chandler was to most of the self-righteous citizens in this town where people didn't forget. Ever.

He crouched to pick up a rock, rubbed his thumb over the river-smooth stone, then slung it out where the water was calm, counting as it skipped across the mirrored surface leaving ripples in its wake.

Five skips. *Not bad for a skinny-assed kid who can't do nothin' right.* Well, ol' Uncle Verne wouldn't be bad-mouthing anyone ever again…not from under six feet of Texas clay.

Verne's saving grace was that he'd moved in after Jake's mom had died. If he hadn't, Jake would've been shipped off to foster care somewhere.

In retrospect…it might've been a better choice.

He hauled in a long breath. He'd thought he'd put all that behind him, but in four short weeks, it all came back in spades.

The crunch of tires on gravel made him turn.

"Yo, Jake!"

He looked up and saw his buddy, Luke, waving from his pickup.

"I tried calling. You didn't answer."

"What's up?"

"One last invitation to come for dinner tonight."

Jake squinted against the morning sun, then made a shield with his hand. Luke didn't give up easily. "Thanks. I appreciate it, but—I've got other plans."

"Yeah?" Luke got out of the truck and headed toward Jake, Stetson shading his eyes. "What plans?" he said in a Texas drawl as long as his legs.

"Just plans." Jake would have liked to spend Christmas Day with Luke's family, but knowing his friend's mom, she'd invite half the town and, considering his reception so far, he didn't feel much like chatting up the neighbors. "Besides, it's family time."

"You're family."

"Dude, everyone is family to your mom."

Luke grinned. "That's true. But she thinks you're special."

Lucy Chisum was one of the few who hadn't condemned Jake for his mother's so-called sins… or for his penchant for getting into trouble, and sometimes taking Luke along with him.

"Besides," Luke added, "we've got a lot of catching up to do. You've been gone a long time."

"Thanks. I'll take a rain check."

"You sure?"

"I'm sure." Even after years apart, they were good enough friends that Luke knew when not to push it.

Reaching down, Luke grabbed a stone and sent it skipping across the water.

Jake picked one up and tossed it from hand to hand. "How much you got on it?"

"Same as always." Luke tugged the brim of his hat, then reached down for another stone.

The bet they'd had as kids—winner picked the pocket and won whatever money was in it.

"You're on." Jake dropped his rock and found another, making sure it was smooth and flat, then leaned sideways and squinted. He lifted a finger to test the wind, then let 'er rip. The stone skipped once, hovered for a fraction of a second and then sank. "Shit."

"Okay." Luke elbowed Jake. "Move aside and let the master take over." With one sure flick of the wrist, Luke's stone glided over the water, skipping at least six times. He crossed his arms. "Hot damn! I still have it."

"The hell you do. I'm just out of practice. Which one?"

Luke pointed to Jake's right front pocket, frowning as Jake pulled out an empty flap of fabric and shrugged.

"You knew that all along."

Jake grinned.

Luke got quiet and rubbed his chin. "So," he said. "You given any more thought to staying?"

*That* again. Cole Lawry, Brady Carrick and Luke had been nagging him to fix up the old Wild Card Saloon ever since he arrived. Even Blake Smith, a relative newcomer to the Wild Bunch had gotten on the wagon. Not one poker game in four weeks had passed without one of them bringing it up.

Fact was, he'd never thought about staying. The only thought he *ever* had about the town that spit him out was finding some way to get even. "Excuse me." Jake tugged on one ear, then the other. "Something must be wrong with my hearing because the words comin' out of your mouth are the same ones over and over, like a broken record."

"That's because it's a great idea."

"Maybe for someone else. I don't need another business. Especially one that—" Jake stopped. His feelings about the Wild Card were his own. His friends only knew what he'd let them know. "Especially when it would be a losing proposition. No one in this town is going to come to a bar I own."

Luke waved a hand, his enthusiasm

with the idea unbridled. "Forget the townspeople. The Wild Card's history as an old poker palace could bring in a lot of tourists. More and more, the hill country is getting known as a great vacation spot. With a little promotion, you'd be raking in the dough."

"I don't need the dough." *Tellmell.com*, the Internet business he'd started ten years ago, had gone ballistic, affording him to do just about anything he wanted. And now that his junior partner had taken over the day-to-day management, Jake had the time, too. But renovating the Wild Card wasn't even on his radar.

Luke shifted his stance, a gleam in his eye. "Okay. Then think about how renovating the place would torque the old attitudes."

Jake laughed outright. Luke knew all the right buttons to push. It would feel mighty good to take a jab at the high and mighty who still ran River Bluff, but his business decisions were based on logic and facts. Not emotion.

"Tourists?" Jake glanced around. "They must be invisible."

"It's winter. They'll be here when it warms up."

Jake sucked air through his teeth and shook his head. "And that's the problem. *I* won't be."

Luke's mouth quirked up on one side. "If you get all the guys to help out, it's as good as done. Blake has connections with contractors in San Antonio, Cole's starting his own construction company and his carpentry skills would—"

Jake held up his hands in a time-out signal, then checked his watch. "Don't you have family to get home to? A big turkey dinner to eat?"

Shrugging, Luke said, "Yep. Now that you mention it, I do." He started up the riverbank, then turned back to Jake again. "You've got friends. Remember that."

"I know. Thanks."

They stood for a moment in uncomfortable silence, before Luke finally said, "Okay then. If you get done early with whatever it is you're doing, c'mon by."

Jake gave him a military salute. "Don't forget poker. We're switching this week from Wednesday because of the holidays."

"Do we have enough players? Cole's still in Oregon with Tessa, y'know."

"We've got seven. That's enough." More was better, but being short a few guys wouldn't stop the diehards from playing—and Jake was one of them. The Wild Bunch was the one thing he'd missed about River Bluff.

"Great." Luke gave Jake a thumbs-up. "I'll be there."

When Luke was gone, Jake glanced downstream to the Bald cypress in the wetlands at the river's edge. Past it, the Wild Card Saloon crouched on the bank where the water curved south like a fat, silver snake. Even though the Wild Bunch had helped fix one part of the roof and cleaned up the apartment in the back, the old honky-tonk bar showed years of neglect.

The Western facade on the front of the building facing the river, sloped down on one side making it look as if it were sinking into the earth. The bar section, shut down after his mom died, encompassed most of the first floor and had stood empty for years. Except for the Wild Bunch games in his absence, he was given to understand.

As he walked along the riverbank toward the dilapidated building, he came across the old bigtooth maple his mom had called "the wishing tree."

When he was very little, she'd told him that if he laid his hand on the tree, closed his eyes and made an unselfish wish, it would come true. He must've made a hundred wishes on the tree and, aside from his runaway dog returning, none ever did.

He reached out and traced the edges of the heart he'd carved in seventh grade, the bark rough against his fingertips.

He'd been a dreamer back then. The initials he'd carved in the center of the heart were about as hopeful as any twelve-year-old kid could get. *R.D.* Rachel Diamonte had been out of his league.

The same year he'd carved the heart, he'd made a wish that his mother would get well.

Jake swallowed a lump in his throat.

Pulling up his collar against another sharp gust of wind, he continued walking through the weeds. Closer to the bar, he saw a black Lincoln Town Car parked on the road near the *For Sale* sign he'd put up. The windows on the vehicle were tinted dark, so he couldn't tell if there was anyone inside.

"Excuse me."

Jake turned. A middle-aged man in a navy-blue suit approached from the west side of the building. He'd apparently been looking over the place. No one he recognized.

"I'm looking for Jake Chandler."

"You got him. What can I do for you?" Stepping up onto the weathered board-walk, Jake noticed the man's spit-shined shoes, the straight-from-the-cleaners starched shirt and the perfectly matched tie that looked as if it was choking the life out of him.

"I'm Mike Dempsey, with the Flanni-gan and Fitch Law Firm in San Antonio." He shook hands with Jake, then gestured to the sign. "A client of mine is interested in your property, and since I was in the area, I thought I'd take a chance you might be here."

Interest was good. He hadn't had any yet. Still, he wasn't going to get too excited. The building might not be worth much, but the five acres of land it sat on were prime.

"Who's your client?"

The attorney raised his chin a hair. "I have an offer in my briefcase. I'll get it and then we can talk." Dempsey started toward the car.

Jake's skin prickled at the brush-off.

An offer without even seeing the place? "You didn't answer my question."

The attorney stopped and turned to face Jake again. "I assure you the offer is more than the property is worth."

"That's great. Who's your client?"

Jake saw a muscle near the guy's eye twitch, but his expression didn't give away anything. "My client is an LLC, a limited liability corporation."

Jake waited.

"Wade Barstow," the attorney finally said.

Jake's blood rushed. Wade Barstow. The man everyone in town thought Lola Chandler had slept with. The man everyone in town *believed* was Jake's father. Hell, he'd heard the story so often, he believed it himself.

His mother had always told him the stories weren't true, that his dad had skipped out after hearing his mother was pregnant, and he'd wanted to believe her. But over the years, whenever Barstow's name had come up, he'd seen the way her eyes lit up.

The only thing Jake knew for certain was that he'd never known his father, and his father didn't want to know him.

"I'll get the papers," the attorney said.

As he watched Dempsey head for his car, Jake's heart began to pump like a piston. Wade Barstow wanted his property. Was he afraid Jake might ask questions? Was he embarrassed that Jake was still in River Bluff? Did Barstow feel guilty he'd never acknowledged him?

"Wait," Jake called out. He needed time to think.

The man turned.

"I have to be somewhere," Jake said. "So you'll have to come back at another time."

Dempsey grinned from ear to ear. "I think you'll change your mind after you've seen the offer."

Barstow practically owned the whole town and now he wanted the saloon. Or did he want the property because he wanted Jake gone?

Jake crossed his arms and wondered what kind of money Barstow thought would be enough to get the bad seed out of town.

Dempsey came back and handed the papers to Jake. "It's a good price. Is there someplace we can sit to discuss it?"

One quick glance at the figure listed on the top of the sheet told Jake what he wanted to know. "No. Like I said, I've got to go. If you want to come back with a real offer after the holidays, give me a call."

The attorney opened his mouth to say something, but apparently thought better of it and walked away. A few minutes later, Jake heard the car door slam and then the sound of the motor and spitting gravel as the guy hauled ass outta there.

Jake went inside the small apartment at the back of the bar where he and his mother had lived. The four rooms had been part of the old bar at one time, but in Texas it was illegal to play poker in a bar, so a section of the apartment in back had been made into a poker room.

Apparently Jake's uncle had allowed the Wild Bunch to continue playing in the room—for a price. That fit. Jake remembered his uncle would've done almost anything to get his next bottle of whiskey. Except work.

Jake took a Shiner out of the ancient fridge, walked to the window and opened the beer. He gulped a swig. So Barstow wanted him gone. How about that.

A spider crack in the glass distorted the gray branches of the cypress at the edge of the water, making them look like gnarly dark claws.

Barstow must think he was incredibly stupid.

He downed the beer on the third pass, then squeezed the empty can until it dented in the middle.

Well, Barstow could want him gone from here to hell and back. This time, he wasn't going to be run out of town by anyone.

When he left River Bluff again—and he would—it was going to be on his own terms.

ROUNDING THE CURVE in the road, Rachel felt a wave of nostalgia wash over her. She'd been gone a long time. Since college. She hadn't known how much she missed the hill country until right this minute. And somehow, that made her feel a little less desperate. River Bluff was familiar. Comfortable.

And a rueful reminder of what she'd done.

*You can't change the past*. When she reached Main Street, Rachel saw that the old River Bluff Hotel had been renovated, but the church, Harry's Hardware store and the Longhorn Café all looked the same.

She smiled.

It was three days past Christmas and decorations still adorned most of the buildings. There were twinkle lights wrapped around the black lampposts, which were draped in swags. The decorations would stay up well past New Year's Day, she remembered. At night all the lights would glitter. She felt a warmth in her chest just thinking about it. There was something magical about the town during the holidays.

She glanced back at Zoe, asleep in her car seat. She couldn't wait to see her daughter's reaction to the glitter.

She parked diagonally a few spaces down from the café. She'd go inside when Zoe woke up and ask Eddie—if he still owned the café—whether he knew of any work in town. If she could find something…anything…she wouldn't be quite so dependent when she went to her mother's for help.

The prospect made her shiver. She hadn't talked to her mother in a year, but she had a pretty good idea what kind of reception she was going to get.

If she had any other choice…

*Well, you don't. So stop thinking about it.* Sighing, she let her head loll against the headrest, the warmth of the sun soothing her ragged nerves. She hadn't had a full night's sleep in what seemed like forever, and driving so many hours had made her sleepy.

She was dozing off when she heard a loud thump and her eyes flew open.

A man in a black leather jacket—a man she'd know anywhere—stood in front of the café. For a second, she thought she was dreaming.

She inched down in her seat, hoping he wouldn't look her way. But she couldn't stop watching him. Jake Chandler was the last person she'd expected to see. What was he doing back in River Bluff?

He zipped his coat, then turned and headed for the Harley a couple of spaces away.

Just as he had years ago, Jake didn't walk, he sauntered. As if he hadn't a care in the world.

He raised his head to put on his helmet and her breath hitched. Suddenly she was transported to that day he'd given her a ride home—the wind in her face and the scent of leather in her nostrils as she clung to him on the back of his motorcycle.

She pretended to look for something on the seat. Had he seen her? Recognized her? In her peripheral vision she saw someone in the doorway of the café.

Oh, geez! Stefi Martin. The once-upon-a-time Barbie look-alike was watching Rachel watch Jake. Stefi flashed Rachel a toothy smile, but just as quickly redirected her gaze to Jake and waved at him with what seemed like intimacy.

Jake gave Stefi a barely perceptible nod, kicked his motorcycle into gear and then roared away with a loud engine backfire.

Zoe shrieked.

"It's okay, honey," Rachel said as she reached back to touch her daughter's tiny hand. "Don't cry."

Zoe screamed even louder. Getting out of the van, Rachel forced a smile to acknowledge Stefi and then went to Zoe's side, soothing her until she calmed down.

When Zoe was quiet again, Rachel unlatched the baby carrier part of the car seat, grabbed the handle and headed into the café.

Amazon-tall Stefi held the door open. "I knew that was you, Rachel Diamonte. But you do look different."

Clutching the carrier, Rachel squeezed by the woman whose boobs suddenly seemed as large as footballs. "It has been a while."

"Right. How long? Ten years? It's nice to see you again."

Taken aback by Stefi's friendliness, Rachel said, "You, too, Stefi, and it's five years. I was here for my dad's funeral. A day that changed everything."

"Cute baby," the other woman said, though she'd barely glanced at Zoe.

Just as well. Rachel didn't feel like answering the inevitable questions.

Stefi went behind the counter, took out a couple of cups and poured some coffee. Motioning Rachel to sit, she said, "I'm filling in this morning. Jenny had something to take care of and Eddie's gone to San Antonio."

Rachel positioned Zoe on the floor at her side with a toy and then sat on a stool.

"Jenny?"

"Yeah. Oh, you wouldn't know her, would you? She moved here with her mother a couple of years ago." Not bothering to explain any further, Stefi added, "I like your new hairstyle. I'd cut mine, too, but every guy I meet seems to like long hair."

Rachel touched her hair—in need of a touch-up and trim. She didn't think of her shoulder-length, feathered style as short, but there was no point in saying so. "It's easier this way."

"What do you think of your mom's new beau?"

*A beau?* Her mom had a boyfriend? "Uh—I'm not giving opinions on that one," she said, wondering if anyone knew how long it had been since she'd seen her mom. Or even talked to her for that matter. On the other hand, in a town the size of River Bluff, everyone knew everything. One of the drawbacks. Although Sarah Diamonte wouldn't let anyone know about the rift between them because she was obsessed with appearances.

"There hasn't been a word about you coming to visit," Stefi said.

"That's because it's a surprise visit, so don't ruin it for me, okay?"

Stefi took a sip of coffee, her gaze making Rachel uncomfortable. "Yeah, sure. I guess you saw Jake, huh. Bet you didn't know *he* was going to be in town."

Rachel's cheeks warmed. Stefi hadn't changed. She was as direct as always. "No. I didn't know," she said, trying to sound matter-of-fact.

"Do you think he still hates you?"

Rachel snapped her head up. What did Stefi know about anything?

"I don't mean he should or anything. But you know men. They hold grudges."

Yes, she knew men. And some did hold grudges. Alex, her ex-husband. Her so-called high-school ex-friend, Kyle Barstow. And Jake.

Jake was the only one who had good reason.

But men weren't the only ones to hold grudges. Her mother did, too. A grudge big enough that she'd never even seen her own granddaughter.

Rachel glanced at Zoe, sweet and innocent and pure, and in that moment, every protective instinct in Rachel rose to the fore. She lifted her chin and looked directly at the woman in front of her.

"Well, you know what, Stefi? Men can just go to hell."

# *CHAPTER TWO*

OKAY. I CAN DO THIS.

Rachel made the turn into the driveway to her mother's new house. She could do this. She had to.

By now, her mother might've heard from someone else that Rachel was in town and would be furious that she'd been the last to know.

Nothing Rachel could do about that now. She was here to ask for forgiveness…and a favor. She'd promise her mother anything.

Her stomach ached at the thought.

When facing bankruptcy, Rachel had asked her mother for a loan to keep her business afloat. She'd been devastated when her mother refused and told

Rachel she'd made her own mess and she'd have to get herself out of it.

Sarah Diamonte rejected anything less than perfection.

Rachel held Zoe tightly in her arms. Maybe seeing Zoe would spark grand-motherly emotions.

Girding her resolve, Rachel rang the bell. Seconds later, the door opened and Sarah stood on the other side in white slacks and blue silk blouse, her golden hair coiffed.

"Hello, Mother."

Sarah's expression remained fixed.

"I tried to call, but—couldn't get through. I'm sorry to surprise you like this."

Her mother pursed her lips. "Surprise? Everyone in town knows you're here."

"I'm sorry. As I say, I tried calling but—"

"Your gallivanting around town with that baby has everyone talking."

Rachel's spine went rigid. "Her name is Zoe."

Sarah backed away. "You know what I mean."

Unfortunately, she did. But having learned early on to read the woman's moods, Rachel knew Sarah was on the defensive…and she'd say anything to make it seem as if she was the victim.

Rachel couldn't let it get to her. "Yes, I do. I'm sorry. Can we please come inside so we can talk?"

Her mother opened the door a little wider, then waited while Rachel picked up Zoe's seat and stepped in. Not long after Rachel's father died, Sarah had sold the home Rachel had grown up in— the home where Rachel's father had been the buffer between the two women.

Rachel walked through the marble-floored foyer and into the living room to tuck her tired little girl back into her car seat. She'd barely gotten Zoe in before the child fell asleep. Rachel sat on the edge of the couch next to her.

Sarah glided across the room and came to rest on a chair opposite Rachel.

Nodding toward Zoe, she asked, "Does she do that all the time?"

"Do what?"

"Sleep. Is that part of her—problem?"

A nerve near Rachel's right eye twitched. "She's napping. She always naps after she's eaten. It's nothing to do with Down syndrome." And if her mother had taken ten minutes to learn anything about the condition, she'd know that.

"She's fine, Mother. Aside from a few areas where she needs special attention, she's a healthy, happy baby."

Sarah reached out, adjusting the candle on the end table next to her. "How long do you plan to be in town?"

Her mother's voice was flat, as if she were talking to a stranger. The falling out they'd had after Rachel's father died five years ago, was just one of many disagreements. But it was the one that severed the relationship so that it had taken every shred of Rachel's strength to call and ask for help with the bankruptcy, during her divorce. Her mother's refusal had felt like a death blow. And now here she was again. Desperate.

"I need to talk to you about that—and maybe it would be better to do it over tea or something."

"I'm sorry, I don't have much time. I have plans for this afternoon and tonight."

So…there wasn't going to be any way to ease into it. "Okay. Well, do you remember the letter I wrote you about the divorce?"

"How could I forget?"

Right. "Well, it was final a few months ago, but Alex left town before the court date. Consequently, he's never paid a dime in child support. When he left, he took all the money in our checking and savings, which left me with no money to finish the accounts I was designing for. Money my clients had paid me. As you know, I had to file bankruptcy and my reputation as an interior designer was ruined. I've been trying to manage since then, but…"

Her mother didn't say a word. Didn't even nod to acknowledge that she'd heard.

Rachel's mouth was dry. "I—thought I could start fresh in River Bluff where I know some people, and I was hoping you'd let me and Zoe stay with you until I can get on my feet again."

Sarah blinked. Her mouth twisted scornfully. "You don't come home for years and now you just pop in and say you want to stay here?"

Rachel's heart pounded. Her hands started to sweat. "I don't know what else to do." She rubbed her palms on her thighs. "Do you remember when you told me that I'd have to suffer the conse- quences of my actions?" Rachel cast her gaze downward. "Well, I'm suffering right now. But I can't let my child suffer, too. I need your help. Your granddaughter needs your help. Not for long. Just until I can get work and find a place of my own."

Sarah looked to Rachel, then to Zoe. "You knew she'd have problems, yet you had her anyway. You knew Alex didn't want children, yet you went ahead anyway."

Rachel rubbed her aching stomach. "You're right. You were absolutely right all along. I knew what the pregnancy would cost me. I take full responsibility for that decision." And there wasn't a question in her mind that she'd do the exact same thing all over again. "But I didn't know Alex would destroy my business."

For the first time, Rachel thought she saw a hint of compassion in her mother's eyes.

Sarah lifted her chin. "As I said, I have plans for this evening. It is the holiday season, after all." She stood. "I'll be right back. I have to make a phone call."

Stunned at her mother's abrupt departure, Rachel felt paralyzed. Tears welled in her eyes. She had known this was going to be hard, but the reality far surpassed any scenario she'd imagined.

Worse yet, she felt like a scared kid

again, hiding in the dark closet to escape her mother's tirades. Anxious… fearful, never knowing when the boom would drop, never knowing what she'd done wrong or what she could do to be a better person.

Remembering the set of unreasonable expectations she'd had to live up to in the past, a dire feeling of hopelessness enveloped Rachel.

In the nine months before Zoe's birth, and the eight months after, Rachel had finally come to value herself for who she was and not for who other people wanted her to be. Funny how it took losing everything to see that.

Her mother returned, a jacket over her arm, a purse in one hand and a fistful of crisp bills in the other. "Here," Sarah said, shoving the money at Rachel. "That should help."

Rachel's mouth dropped open. Her chest constricted as if someone had tightened a vise around it.

"I can't have you here," Sarah said

before Rachel could respond. "I'm seeing someone and he stays here sometimes. I can't have dirty diapers and formula all over the place."

Rachel stared at the money in her palm, then at her mother. "You want me—us—to leave?"

Ice-blue eyes stared back at Rachel. "You made the choice, Rachel. You made it six years ago when you married Alex against my wishes. You made the choice again when you told me at your father's funeral how unhappy I'd made him and it was my fault he'd found another woman. The only reason you want to stay here is because you're broke and have no place else to go."

The sharp edge in her mother's voice cut deep, more than mere words. But everything she said was true.

"Well, now you're not broke anymore. There's enough money for a trip to San Antonio and a few nights in a motel. I'm sure you can find a job there."

Rachel slowly rose to her feet, too

stunned to speak. She steadied herself with one hand on the arm of the couch, while reaching for the handle on Zoe's seat with the other.

She wanted to say something, something important, to somehow put to rest the culmination of a lifetime of hurt between them. But the words crashed together in her head and never made it to her mouth.

"I'm leaving now," Sarah said. "I'll need to lock the door after you."

BITING BACK TEARS, Rachel glanced in the rearview mirror to make sure no cars were behind, then pulled off the road at a rest stop and killed the engine. Hugging the steering wheel, she buried her face in her arms and finally let the tears flow. *Oh, God. What now?*

A sharp wail from the backseat reminded Rachel that Zoe's needs were her priority. She got out of the van and glanced about for facilities. None. Only a rotted picnic table and a broken bench.

She wiped away the tears with her sleeve, opened the side of the old VW bus, slipped in next to Zoe in her car seat and shut the door.

"It's okay, sweetie. I'll think of something." Sure she would.

Zoe puckered her lips, her big blue eyes getting even bigger when Rachel pulled a jar of food from the thermal bag. Feeding Zoe required time and patience, but it was necessary to her development. "You're hungry, aren't you? Mommy shouldn't have waited so long." Zoe registered her delight with a squeal and some spit bubbles.

Putting off Zoe's lunch until they reached Rachel's mother's had been a mistake. She should have known. But the way she felt about her own daughter, she couldn't have imagined any mother turning her child away. No matter how angry she was. If Rachel's father had been there, they'd be sleeping in warm beds tonight. But he wasn't. And they were alone.

"I wish your grandpa could be here to see you, Zoe. He'd love you to pieces. He would've bought you lots and lots of presents for Christmas. And then on Christmas morning, he would've sat on the floor with you and played and played until you were tired and couldn't play anymore."

Rachel sighed, feeling a deep sense of loss. Her father had been the only person who'd loved her unconditionally. Even now, after five years, the pain felt as fresh as if it were yesterday.

"But he watches you from heaven, Zoe. Like your very own guardian angel."

Rachel hadn't had a Christmas like that in eons. Certainly not many while married to Alex. Four days ago on Christmas Eve, she'd stuffed Zoe's stocking with all the little things she'd made for her. A sock monkey with button eyes and a fuzzy kitten cut of yarn. Then, the day after Christmas, and using the money she'd gotten from selling the last of her furniture and her leather coat, they'd left Chicago.

River Bluff was a place where family values still meant something. She could make a good life for Zoe here and that's all that mattered.

She spooned a bite of vegetables into Zoe's mouth and watched her spit it out just as fast, smiling as if she'd done something wonderful. As Rachel lifted the next spoonful, a silver Tahoe whizzed by on the highway, then came to a screeching stop, backed up and pulled in next to them.

A woman got out. Probably someone who saw Rachel's beat-up bus and thought she was in trouble. Watching the woman approach, Rachel opened the window. "I'm not having car trouble if that's what you're thinking. I just stopped for a break."

The woman bent to peer inside. For a moment, she just looked, then her eyes widened. "Rachel?"

Familiar short auburn curls poked

from the woman's fuzzy stocking cap. "Becky?"

A wide, bright smile told Rachel she was right. Sweet Becky Lynn—that's what everyone in high school had called the sheriff's bookish daughter. Wholesome and pretty, Becky didn't look bookish anymore. She no longer wore glasses and there wasn't a freckle in sight.

"Uh-huh. I'm on my way to the clinic." She craned her neck to peek inside. "Oh, my. You have a baby."

"This is my daughter, Zoe," Rachel said proudly. "She's eight months old."

"Wow, you started late, huh. I have a son, Shane, who's fifteen."

Rachel smiled. "I didn't start late— you started early."

They laughed together, and Rachel watched Becky's expression for a reaction when she looked at Zoe. Some people showed surprise, but never said anything. Others came right out and asked what was wrong with her.

"She's adorable," Becky said.

"I think so, but then I might be a little biased."

Becky nodded, then cooed at Zoe. Rachel suddenly wished they had been better friends in school. But she'd been so busy living up to her mother's expectations, she hadn't had time for anything that wasn't on her mother's list. Now, after being gone for so long, Rachel felt even more like an outsider.

"I guess you're going to stay at your mom's for a while, huh?" Becky said as she surveyed the back of the van, jampacked with what was left of Rachel's worldly possessions.

"Actually, no," Rachel said as she scraped the bottom of the jar and spooned the rest into Zoe's little bird mouth. "I want to find a place of my own."

In her peripheral vision, Rachel saw Becky draw back in surprise. Staying with relatives is what people did in small towns like River Bluff.

"It's a long story," Rachel added.

"Oh," Becky said sympathetically. "Anything I can do to help?"

Rachel wished. "Only if you know someone who needs an interior designer," she said facetiously. As far as Rachel knew, the only person in River Bluff who'd ever use a designer was her mother. Or maybe Brady Carrick's mother, Angela.

Rachel had heard from Stefi that Angela was hitting the bottle pretty heavily these days, so it wasn't likely she was doing any decorating.

Rachel prepared some apple juice and helped Zoe work the straw. She was doing well, the doctor had said. She was a high functioning Down syndrome child and at the top of the development chart.

She saw Becky studying her left hand.

"Zoe's father and I are divorced."

Becky's brows met in the middle, then she nodded her understanding and waved her own ringless hand. "Me, too."

"I'm sorry. Who did you marry?"

"Danny Howard. It was great for a while, but—" She shrugged. "I guess you know how that goes."

The last Rachel knew, Becky was head over heels in love with Luke Chisum— even after the infamous episode when Rachel had overheard some of the guys remembering how they'd laid bets on Luke to ask Becky out on their first date. Rachel had felt a duty to tell Becky, and then Becky hadn't talked to her for at least a month. "I hate to ask—but did you and Luke ever make up?"

Becky looked away. "That was a long time ago. We were kids."

A long time or not, the wistful tone in Becky's voice gave Rachel the distinct impression Becky wasn't entirely over Luke. The old saying about never forgetting your first love was all too true.

"Oh, hey." Becky snapped her fingers. "Do you remember Jake Chandler? He's back in River Bluff, and I heard through the grapevine he might be renovating the

Wild Card Saloon. You could go out and see him and find out if he needs an interior designer. I bet he'd be surprised to see you."

Surprised, maybe. But not pleased. Becky had to be the only person in town who didn't know Jake hated her. Either that, or she'd forgotten. Odd that Stefi hadn't mentioned Jake might need help. Then again, maybe not. It looked as if Stefi had first dibs on Jake.

"We didn't hang out in the same circles," Rachel said. "Besides, he probably needs carpenters, not a designer. I doubt he'd—"

"Maybe I can get some information for you. Give me your cell phone number and I'll call you when I get the scoop." Becky glanced at her watch. "Oh, man. I've got to go or I'll be late. I'm working at the clinic today. I'm a nurse," Becky explained. "I work part-time there and also at the high school. It's winter vacation for the school kids right now, so I'm at the clinic more often."

A nurse. That's why she hadn't asked about Zoe.

"So, I'll call you?"

"Gosh, that's great, only—my cell phone isn't working right now." Phones didn't work if you didn't pay the bill.

"No problem. You can call me, then." Becky reached into her pocket, pulled out a card and handed it to Rachel.

Rachel sighed as she watched Becky leave, relieved the woman hadn't asked her why she was here. Becky was as sweet as ever, and it felt good to talk to another woman who seemed to understand without having to explain everything.

She kissed Zoe on the forehead, then watched her little girl reach for the stuffed monkey in the seat. Rachel picked it up and playfully touched the toy to Zoe's nose. Zoe giggled with delight. Lord, she loved Zoe so much. How could anyone not?

How could Alex not care about his own daughter? How could her mother not care about either of them?

With Zoe fed and sleeping, she pulled out the money her mother had given her. Enough for a couple of nights at a cheap motel. She shoved the bills back into her purse, got out, slipped into the driver's seat and drove back toward town.

Because Alex's insurance was still in effect and she could continue it on her own afterward, she had more than three months before she had to apply for state funding to help out—if she needed it. Zoe didn't have many of the problems typical of Down children. All she needed was a job that paid enough money to keep a roof over their heads and food in their stomachs. Admitting she'd failed again—just as her mother predicted—wasn't going to happen.

## CHAPTER THREE

JAKE MUCKED HIS CARDS aside and glanced at the clock. It was nearly 2:00 a.m. Saturday morning already. He'd bet his last stack of chips, and everyone was out of the Texas Hold'em game except his buddies, Brady Carrick and Luke Chisum, who were in a head-to-head. They got nothing on the flop, and it was up to Luke to meet Brady's bet.

Jake sat back and, studying their body language, decided Brady was bluffing because he'd been fingering his chips. Brady had always had the cojones to bluff big-time. Losing his shirt in Vegas was not the reason he was back in River Bluff working for his dad. Jake figured, of all the guys, he might be the only one who knew the whole story about Brady leaving Las Vegas…and why he got so moody sometimes.

After a brief hesitation, Luke met the bet. "Big Brady thinks he's gonna hit on the turn," Luke said, stripping off the shades he'd put on as a joke after Cole's former boss, Ron Hayward, had shown up sporting neon green sunglasses.

Ron had flipped Luke the bird and ignored him the rest of the night.

Brady glanced at his hole cards for the second time, a sign he hadn't connected, or at least not well. But with Brady, you never knew and, tonight, he was on a high because he thought his father might buy a particular racehorse Brady was eager to train.

Harry Knutson, another regular and the owner of the hardware store, flipped the turn card. Luke smiled as if Harry had done him a favor. Jake knew when Luke smiled or started joking around, it meant he had squat. When he got quiet and kicked up his bets, odds were he had a good hand. They all knew what it meant when he pulled his Stetson down on his forehead.

It was Luke's bet and the other players watched intently. Except for Ron, who didn't hold his liquor well and was sloppy drunk again. Though they all drank, there was a line they didn't cross. Ron didn't seem to know that, and Jake guessed he wouldn't last long with the group if he kept it up. But Ed Falconetti was a keeper. He owned the Longhorn Café and between him and Harry, they had the inside track on everything that went on in River Bluff. Especially since Harry's wife ran the only beauty shop in town.

"I need a beer," Luke said, getting up and going to the fridge in the kitchen, an L-shaped extension off Jake's living room where they were playing.

"Tough decision?" Brady needled.

Luke ambled back to the old oak table, set his beer down and took his seat. Leaning back, he stretched out his long legs. "Hell, no," he said, his drawl making hell sound like hail. He lifted the beer to his lips and took a lengthy swig.

"Let's get this over and start a new game," Ron mumbled.

Blake, another regular, and now Cole's new brother-in-law, frowned. "It'll get over when it's over."

Jake grinned. Blake understood the rituals, elevating him a notch in Jake's eyes. And at two in the morning, it wasn't likely they'd start another one.

Brady looked at Luke, took a drink himself, then tapped the Dallas Cowboys bobblehead doll—a white elephant gift he'd received. "You can take as long as you want. The numbers aren't gonna change."

Ignoring him, Luke tipped his hat forward. "All in," he said and shoved his chips to the center of the table.

The muscles in Brady's jaw visibly tightened. Jake was right. Brady had been bluffing. But Jake did a double-take when Brady met the bet. It took all his chips, so if he didn't win, he'd be done.

Maybe he'd read Brady wrong? Maybe he did have a winning hand? Interest aroused, Jake leaned forward, elbows on the table. A pair of eights, a two and a five showed on the table.

Luke grinned, then flipped his hole cards. A pair of aces.

"You better hit on the river," Brady said. "Or you've got a real dead-man's hand." He turned his hole cards faceup. An eight and a Jack, giving him three of a kind, the winning hand at the moment. But that could change instantly on the river.

Luke sobered. He stood, a habit he had when it was all or nothing. With a fifty-dollar buy-in, the winner's take would be big, but then money wasn't the reason any of them played. Brady leaned back, showing not the slightest bit of nerves. Both waited for the river—the card that would make or break one of them.

Harry made a big production, waving one hand over the deck like a magician, then he slowly flipped over an ace.

Luke grinned from ear to ear. "Hot damn!"

Brady shrugged then tossed his cards to the side. "Pure luck."

"Not bad," Jake said. He handed each man his percentage of the winnings.

Ron shoved his chair back, stood and, reaching for the last Christmas cookie on the plate, started singing "Grandma got run over by a reindeer..."

Harry shoved Ron toward the door. "Geez, Ron. My ears hurt."

Jake slugged down the remnants of his beer.

Within a half hour, everyone had gone except Brady and Luke.

"Ron would probably drop out if we amped up the buy-in," Luke said, waving his winnings like a fan. "We could make it a C-note."

"We could," Brady said, "but I won't be playing."

They all knew Brady hadn't been able to find anything to do for a living that equaled his dazzling stint with the Dallas Cowboys—until he started gambling. He'd been good. Really good. But after the tragedy in Vegas, he'd sworn off the tables and hit bottom before he'd come home to work on his father's ranch. The guys didn't talk about what happened to Brady in Vegas any more than they talked about Luke's stint in Iraq and the injury he refused to take seriously. It seemed the only thing they could talk about was renovating the Wild Card.

"We could give you a discount buy-in," Jake kidded.

Brady tagged him on the arm. "I could give you a sore jaw."

"So, this is what I'm gonna do," Luke injected, tossing his winnings back on the table. "I'm donating my take to the renovation."

Jake scoffed, scooping up the money and stuffing it down the front of Luke's denim shirt. "If I wanted to renovate, I would." He raked a hand through his hair. "Damn. Can't we get through one game without you jokers ragging on me about the Wild Card?"

"Hell, no," Luke said, then headed for the doorway leading into the saloon.

The big double doors were gone and Luke flipped on the makeshift light Jake had rigged up by hanging an old table lamp from one of the beams. It lit up the old mahogany bar, the dance floor—buckled and with big chunks missing—a tied-off electrical cord dangling from the ceiling where a chandelier used to be. The mirror behind the bar had a coating of dust and dirt so thick, the cracked glass was barely visible.

"Look at that wood." Luke gestured toward the bar. "It's an antique. It must be thirty-feet long." He went into the room and swung out his arms. "Look at this place. Everyone will want to come here."

"It's a pile of junk and the bar was twenty-feet long before the corner got hacked off."

Luke walked over, surveying the damage. "It may look like junk now, but it's got potential. The entire building does. You could even rent out Verne's apartment."

"Only if the floors were sound-proofed." The apartment upstairs was in worse condition than the one in the back where Jake was staying. His uncle had been living upstairs until he'd been confined to a wheelchair, and then he'd had to come down. But the place had gone to trash long before that.

"Okay, a poker room then. It's got a separate entrance and everything."

"It would be easier to raze it and start over," Jake said.

Brady propped a foot on one of the boxes, his arm across his knee. "You can't raze it," he said incredulously. "There's history here. Going back generations."

"It was built in the forties with recycled lumber and chewing gum. It's not going to qualify for the historic-building register." Jake picked up a piece of stained glass, part of a window, still in its frame. Still nice. He might take it with him when he left.

"My dad and his friends are always talking about the great times at the Card," Luke continued. "You reopen this place and they'd be first in line at the door."

"Yep. My dad might come back, too," Brady said. "He's always talking about the good ol' days."

Yeah. Both Brady's and Luke's fathers had been regulars. Along with Wade Barstow. "That would go over big with some of the women in town," Jake said with no small amount of sarcasm. Except for Luke's mom, the women in that elite group had treated Jake and his mother like outcasts.

"That was years ago," Brady said. "And if you didn't want to do it yourself, you could hire a manager to run the place. I'm tellin' you, it could be a real gold mine."

"So why don't one of you guys buy it?"

Brady looked at Luke. Luke looked at Brady. They both turned to Jake. "Because we want you to stay," they said practically in unison.

Jake shook his head. "You're both drunk. You should call a cab."

"A cab?" Brady repeated.

Jake grinned and threw up his hands. "Okay, that shows *I've* had one too many." He hadn't been counting, but he knew *he'd* had too much to drive anywhere.

Brady got out his car keys and jangled them in front of Jake. "I'm fine. I had two beers the whole night."

Luke cracked his knuckle and laughed. "Brady's still trying to show his folks he's responsible."

"At least I'm not stupid enough to drive under the influence, like some people I know."

Jake smiled at their banter…and at how there was always some truth under the jokes.

"You're riding with me," Brady told Luke. No suggestion there.

Luke ignored him and turned to Jake. "Just so you know, we're ready to help with the renovation any time you're ready." He tagged Brady on the shoulder. "Isn't that right?"

Just as Brady opened his mouth to respond, Jake covered his ears and started humming.

"And one more thing that just might put you over the edge," Luke said, loudly. "I heard Rachel Diamonte's back."

Jake was still covering his ears when he kicked the door shut behind them.

MORNING CAME TOO SOON and the hammer inside Jake's skull pounded a half-dozen times for every drink he'd had the night before. Dang. He never had more than a couple of beers when he played poker. He should know better.

He glanced at the clock and rolled over again for a few more winks. But just as he was drifting off, he heard a knock at the door. It couldn't have been very loud, but it sounded like thunder in his head. Who the hell would come out here at eight on a Saturday morning?

*Dempsey?* The attorney was the only one who'd wanted to talk to Jake, but he'd told the guy when he called yesterday that he had to wait until after the New Year's holiday. Apparently he didn't understand English.

Jake covered his head with a pillow, feeling no compulsion to answer the door.

Another knock, only this time louder. Dammit. He shoved back the quilt and got to his feet. The room swirled. Slowly he bent to pick up his jeans and, with one hand on the dresser for balance, he struggled into his pants.

The knocking stopped, and Jake sat on the bed, glad whoever it was had given up. Then he heard the door squeak. Someone was coming inside! No way. Jake surged out of the bedroom, his adrenaline pumping. The door was open only a crack. All he could see was a shoulder. A woman's shoulder.

He pulled the door open all the way.

"Hello, Jake."

He felt as if he'd been punched in the gut.

RACHEL SMILED. She couldn't tell if the expression on Jake's face was surprise or disgust, but it didn't matter. She was on a mission.

There was money enough for only one more night at the motel.

Begging Jake for work was the last thing she wanted to do. But with Zoe's welfare at stake, her pride didn't matter. Not one iota. She'd come early to make sure she found him at home, but…

"I'm sorry if I woke you, and I know I'm probably the last person you want to see—but can we talk? It's important."

He stood there, bare chested, eyes bloodshot and his Levi's unbuttoned at the waist. His rather long dark hair looked as if someone had taken a Weed-whacker to it. The stale scent of beer told her why.

"Important to who?"

Right. What was she thinking? Her blood pressure spiked. If she could just get him to listen…. "To both of us."

He stood in the doorway, one hand on the door and one hand on the frame on the opposite side, as if making a barrier to keep her out. She could almost feel his animosity. She took a deep breath.

"I heard you're renovating the Wild Card and you might need—some help. I'm a trained and experienced interior designer and—and I know quite a bit about renovations." Her lips were dry, her throat parched. "I need a job and you need a—someone with my expertise. We could help each other out."

Silence.

"On a professional level."

He looked confused…or curious….or maybe he just hated her too much to say anything. She clenched her hands, digging her fingernails into her palms.

*Leave.* She wanted to. Then she glanced at Zoe, still asleep in her carrier a foot away from the door where Jake couldn't see her.

"Why would I hire *you?*" His voice was low, his words succinct.

Why, indeed? She shoved her hair back from her face. "Because I'm good at what I do. You wouldn't have to hire someone to drive in from San Antonio every day—and I know what would make the Wild Card a draw for locals and tourists alike."

It was true. Ever since she'd talked to Becky and heard he might be renovating, she'd been thinking of ways to refurbish the old saloon. She had a wealth of ideas and she was good at what she did. Damned good.

He looked puzzled. And when he didn't respond, she added, "You don't have to like me to make a good business deal."

She thought she saw a quick flash of…something…in his eyes. Understanding? No, that would be wishful thinking on her part.

"I'm not renovating. I'm selling the place. Didn't you see the sign?"

"Oh." She felt as if her blood had suddenly drained to her toes. "Yes, I saw it. But I also heard—" She caught a breath, trying not to show her disappointment. "I—I guess I heard wrong."

"I guess you did. Who'd you hear it from?"

She pursed her lips. "Does it matter?"

"Not really. In this town, people say what they want whether it's true or not."

He meant her. She'd told the sheriff she'd seen him at Barstow's the night of the fire. "That's true. And sometimes the truth isn't what it seems."

He didn't say anything after that, but his eyes, the color of smooth cognac, darkened, and she knew he was wondering why she'd ever think he'd hire her for anything.

Her heart thudded at the base of her throat, which suddenly began to close up. Even though it was cold this morning, she felt sweat dampen the blue T-shirt she wore under her sweater. She wanted to pick up her child and run away. Far away.

But, dammit. She *needed* a job. *This* job. She couldn't leave without letting him know how knowledgeable she was. How hard working.

Swallowing as she drew air into her lungs, she pulled herself up. "The thing is—I'm not only a designer. I do much more. I pound nails, sweep floors, haul away trash—I'm involved in what I do one-hundred percent."

He was watching her fumble. He probably got enormous satisfaction from watching her grovel.

But if it got her a job, she didn't care. She cleared her throat and went on. "More importantly, I do great design work. I have a portfolio with examples if you'd like to see it."

He didn't answer. Which she figured *was* his answer.

"Well," she said, shrugging. "You know what I do. If you change your mind and decide to renovate, I'd appreciate if you'd keep me in mind." She moistened her parchment-dry lips, then raised a hand. "And one more thing. I work at discount rates."

She turned and was starting to reach for Zoe when he asked, "Why?"

"Why what?"

"Why are you here?"

Puzzled, she scrunched her brows together. "I—I told you. I need a job, and I heard you might need someone."

He waited a second. "I meant in River Bluff."

"Oh." Taken off guard, she waved a hand. "I—got tired of living in Chicago."

He crossed his arms. Eyes narrowed, he looked directly at her. "Why do I think that's a lie? Oh, I know. Because lying is what you do best, isn't it?"

His words cut her like a laser. Her face burned and she couldn't think of a single thing to say. Nothing would change what happened fifteen years ago…or the way he felt about her. Nothing could make it right. "I'm sorry I bothered—"

He closed the door before she finished the sentence.

JAKE STOOD WITH HIS back against the door until he heard an engine and the sound of a vehicle driving away. He didn't look. He didn't want to. Damn. What a way to wake up.

Emotions still churning, he stalked to the kitchen, put on a pot of coffee and then splashed his face with cold water. Who the hell had told her he was renovating?

He dried off, then went to sit at the table, which was still covered with the remnants of last night's poker game—beer bottles, peanuts and chicken bones from the hot wings Eddie had brought from the café. He dumped everything into the trash can.

He heard the coffee pot sputter. The strong scent of chicory permeated the air, reminding him of his mom, how every morning he'd wake up to the aroma.

He glanced around, remembering how his mother had always talked about what she would do to fix up the place if she'd had the money. His hatred for River Bluff had made him forget how much his mother had loved it here, made him forget she'd had big dreams for the Wild Card at one time.

He walked over and found a mug, one of an old set of restaurant dishes from the café that Stefi had talked Ed into giving him, and poured himself a cup. As he did, he glimpsed his reflection in the window. Man, Rachel must've thought he was a bum. Staying here, looking like he did. Reeking of alcohol.

He grabbed a hooded sweatshirt from the back of a chair and slipped it on, then took his coffee outside. He stared at the river, but Rachel's face was all he could see.

He inhaled deeply, dragging cool, crisp air into his lungs. Nice. He drank some coffee, forcing himself to focus on his surroundings. The weather. The coffee. The water. Anything other than Rachel and the supreme gall she'd shown in coming here asking for a job.

*You don't have to like me to do business.* He smiled.

Rachel was right about that. He'd done business with lots of people he didn't like. And he had to admit, renovation had some appeal. It would stick in Barstow's craw even more than if he let the property sit. Yeah. A juvenile thought if ever he had one. But satisfying.

Mug in hand, he strode toward the river. Every morning when he was a kid, he'd come outside and play with the frogs or skip stones. Back then, each day had started out fresh and new...no matter what had happened the day before.

He hadn't felt that way in a very long time.

Something crunched under his boot. He knelt to see charred logs filling the old fire pit where he and his buddies used to hang out after sneaking beer from his uncle's stash—usually after the old sod had passed out.

Way back when, Cole's sister, Annie, had dubbed their misfit group the Wild Bunch. Although now she'd taken to calling them the Not-So-Wild Bunch.

An odd group—Jake and Cole without fathers and both from the wrong side of the tracks, Luke and Brady from wealthy ranching families—and yet they'd all formed a bond that was un-shakable. After Jake's mom died, his friends became his family.

And now—he smiled—the Not-So-Wild Bunch wanted him to stay.

Yeah. Like *that* was going to happen.

He had a thriving business in Califor-nia, enough money to be comfortable, a few good friends, a nice condo and a boat in the San Diego Harbor. Any number of women seemed to want to date the wunderkind of *Tellmell.com,* one of the hottest stocks on the market.

And he was more than happy to take a great many of them up on their offers.

Yet when he'd seen Rachel, he felt like a teenager all over again. Man, he'd acted like such an ass.

He gripped his cup tighter. What the hell brought her back to River Bluff—and to him, of all people—looking for a job?

She'd seemed edgy. Not the self-assured girl she'd been in high school. She still had the Christie Brinkley looks, the bluer-than-blue eyes, the smooth skin and blond hair, except now her hair wasn't long and straight, but shaggy and to her shoulders. She wasn't as slim. And she sure as hell wasn't happy.

He'd fantasized about Rachel Diamonte for three freaking years during high school—until she'd screwed him over. Royally.

And when he saw her standing outside his door this morning…*her* coming to *him*… Man…what a rush! He couldn't have played that one any better if he'd written the script.

Rachel Diamonte. Homecoming queen, cheerleader, class valedictorian.

The person who'd stabbed him in the back without batting an eyelash.

## CHAPTER FOUR

RACHEL TIGHTENED HER grip on the steering wheel, then made the turn onto the road back to town. She'd gone to Bandera to look for work, but on a Saturday the people who do the hiring weren't around.

She had only enough money for one more night at the motel. If she went to San Antonio, she might be able to find a temporary job at a fast-food restaurant... But then what would she do with Zoe?

She couldn't make enough for a month's rent at that kind of job anyway.

God. She must've been out of her mind to think seeing her granddaughter would spark some kind of grandmotherly emotions in Sarah Diamonte.

Rachel had spent her whole life trying unsuccessfully to be what her mother wanted. Marrying Alex might even have been an act of defiance. One that back-fired.

Lost in thought, she felt the steering wheel vibrate and tightened her grip. But it suddenly felt like a jackhammer under her fingers and she heard a loud bang. The van lurched to one side.

Oh, no! She yanked the wheel the opposite way and pumped the brakes, but the van didn't stop. She pulled the emergency brake, heard a loud grinding sound and watched helplessly as they rolled slowly down the embankment, coming to a bumpy stop in the ditch.

She glanced at Zoe.

Zoe was still asleep…and making little snuffling noises as if she might be waking up. Incredible. Absolutely in-credible. Rachel let out a quiet laugh, and then for a moment, she just sat there, clutching the wheel, hands shaking, blood pounding through her veins.

So, what now? She'd already used her spare on the way to Texas and hadn't had the money to get it fixed. But she still had one of those canned air things. No problem. All she had to do is read the directions.

She got out, but left the door ajar so she could also hear Zoe if she cried. She wrinkled her nose at the smell of burned rubber, as she pushed weeds aside to see the damage—a three-inch gash in the side of the tire. Crap.

The air thing wasn't going to work on that. She dropped onto her butt, pulled her knees up and rested her head on her arms.

It was getting dark. Her cell phone didn't work. She was at least four miles from town, on a small country road that wasn't well traveled.

Lord, she didn't know whether to laugh or cry.

But…neither would do any good, and she couldn't just sit there. She *could* drive on the tire. It wouldn't get any flatter. But to do that, she'd have to get out of the ditch first, and she'd ruin the rim if she drove on it. Then she'd have to buy a tire and a rim, which didn't matter because she didn't have money for either one.

On the plus side, River Bluff was a town full of good-hearted people. If Rick was still doing mechanic work, he'd let her pay later.

So, how would she get hold of Rick? She took stock of her surroundings. Waiting for someone to drive by could take hours. She'd taken the shorter route to town not realizing the road was rutted and apparently not well-traveled. Well, she had food for Zoe and diapers and water and blankets and sleeping bags, she'd made sure of that before leaving Chicago. It wasn't as if they'd starve or freeze.

She stood, brushed herself off and climbed the embankment to the road. Not a car in sight.

The December sky looked ominous,

and the chill in the air was biting. It wasn't that late, but night came quickly at this time of the year, and out here where there were no highway lights, the lone flashlight she had in the van wouldn't do much good.

Jake's was about a mile and a half back. One alternative was to walk to his place and use his phone to get help. The other was…well, there wasn't any other except to wait for someone to come along.

She slid into the driver's seat. Zoe was waking up and rubbing her eyes. "Hey, punkin. Did you have a good sleep?" Rachel tried to sound cheery even though her spirit wasn't in it. "I bet you need your diaper changed." She started the van. "It'll be just a minute."

She hit the clutch and shoved the shift into gear, then pressed the gas, lightly at first, then with more pressure. They didn't move an inch. Damn. She gunned the engine. The van lurched forward— then stopped dead. She turned the key again. Nothing. Not even a grinding sound.

Well, why not. Wasn't that how everything was going today? "Okay, munchkin." She got out, opened Zoe's door and unlatched the child's safety belt. Zoe kicked her legs and made more spit bubbles.

Rachel picked Zoe up and felt her warm little body against her own. Her heart melted. Unconditional love. Complete dependence and unconditional love. The thought humbled her.

When she finished changing Zoe, Rachel opened one of the cardboard boxes and pulled out the BabyBjörn backpack. She'd have to pack some things to carry with them, but first things first.

Zoe had a daily routine to strengthen her muscles and help her learn to grip things rather than pushing them, and just because they were traveling, Rachel wasn't going to let it go. Her daughter's special needs provided some challenges, but the blessings far outweighed them.

Whenever she saw Zoe struggling with something that should be easy for a baby her age, she wanted to jump in and help her little girl, do it for her. But she couldn't. Not if she wanted Zoe to ever become self-sufficient. When Zoe had small successes Rachel's motherly pride soared.

Being Zoe's mother had taught Rachel many things, but the most important was patience.

"When we finish here, we're going to take a walk, Zoe. That'll be fun, won't it? We might see some deer, or maybe an armadillo. We're going to call this trip Zoe's big adventure."

The baby squealed, then grabbed a hunk of Rachel's hair.

"Yeah, you think that's even more fun, don't you." Rachel pried her daughter's chubby fingers from her head. "You know what, Zoe? I'm going to think of this as a grand adventure, too."

She had to. Because seeing Jake again would be downright humiliating.

"TUESDAY, AFTER New Year's Day," Jake said, after agreeing on a time to meet with the attorney. He needed a few more days to mull the offer over.

"Where?" After spending New Year's Eve with Brady and Luke in San Antonio, he'd likely need the next day to recover.

"I'll come out there in the afternoon. How's three?"

"I'll be here."

Jake closed his cell phone and set it on the battered table he'd rescued from under a pile of trash in the bar. He rubbed one of the gouges with his thumb and found it smooth from wear. The table had character. Brady and Luke were right. History practically screamed from the stained and dilapidated walls.

He'd spent the first eighteen years of his life here, and as tacky as the little apartment was, he felt as at home as he did in his condo on the water in San Diego.

He could've stayed at the old Frontier

Hotel or the River Bluff Lodge while he was in town, but his past was here. And if he sold the place, he'd close the door on that part of his life.

He glanced around. Every night he'd had to listen to the drunks through his paper-thin bedroom walls.

When he'd really listened, even through the clink of glasses and the country music, he used to recognize the voices. He smiled. He'd heard a hell of a lot.

But what he remembered best was when Woody Wilson came out from San Antonio and sang the blues all night long. Jake would lie in bed and sing along.

Whenever his mom had heard him singing, she'd told him he was so good he could be a famous singer one day if he wanted, and his ten-year-old chest had swelled up like a puffer fish. It hadn't mattered if his voice was good or not. What had mattered was that his mom was proud of him. That she loved him, no matter what.

His phone rang and, flipping it open, he saw Stefi's number. "Hey."

Jake heard music in the background. "What's up?"

"I'm at Eleventh Street. C'mon down."

The Eleventh Street Cowboy Bar in the nearby town of Bandera was probably the only place Jake could go and not get stared at or be whispered about. "Okay. Give me twenty."

If he decided to reopen the Card, he'd be in direct competition with the Cowboy Bar. That could be a problem. But he wasn't going to reopen anything, so why even think about it? He had a life in California. He had no life here.

Fifteen minutes later, he was on the road in the old green pickup he'd bought off the ranch foreman at the Chisum ranch.

Jake was glad to have something to do tonight since his buddies were with their families. Still, he had to be careful with Stefi. She was looking for her fourth husband, and he was leaving this burg as soon as he could. Alone.

He searched for a CD and just as he was sticking it into the Walkman he caught a glimpse of an old VW bus in the ditch. It looked like the one he'd seen parked in front of the Longhorn the day before yesterday.

He slowed, then pulled to a stop on the narrow shoulder and got out.

The sun had already set and in the twilight it was hard to see if anyone was inside. Just as he reached the side door, the window rolled down partway.

Bluer than blue eyes stared back at him, and his heart skipped a jillion beats. He leaned forward. "Are you all right?"

Rachel nodded. "I am now. I didn't think anyone would come along, and I was just about to start walking."

"What happened?"

"A flat tire put me in the ditch."

"Did you call someone?"

"No. My phone—isn't working. So, as I said, I was about to start walking."

"Where were you headed?"

She raised her eyebrows. "I was going

to walk back to your place and ask to use your phone." She paused. "Do you know someone who can help me?"

*Did he know anyone?* What did she think? That he was some kind of hard-ass who wouldn't help a woman in trouble? Especially when she had that desperate look in her eyes. A look that brought out all his strong-man protective feelings. "Yeah. Me. If it's just a tire."

"Well, thanks. That makes me feel a whole lot better."

That sure sounded sarcastic. And the way *he* felt, she didn't have any room to be pushing her luck.

"It's the tire, but it's shredded."

He went around to check it out and noticed the van was packed full. "Where's your spare?"

Her mouth crooked up on one side. "That's another problem. It's already in use. And the motor won't start, either."

The vulnerability in her voice made him want to…to protect her somehow.

"Do you have a phone I could use?" she asked.

He handed her his cell.

As she took it, Rachel saw him look away. He wanted to help her about as much as he wanted to take up knitting. "Do you know if Rick is still doing mechanic work?" She rolled down the window the rest of the way, noting his surprise when he looked back and registered Zoe in her arms.

"Uh, yeah, he's still around, but I heard he's out of town for the holidays."

Great. Now what was she going to do? Jake shifted his feet and glanced down the road and back again. Then he turned and walked away. She started. He wouldn't just leave her there, would he? He strode purposefully to his truck, looked into the bed, then returned.

"I don't have what I need to get you out of the ditch. But I can give you a ride wherever you're going."

She gave him a wobbly smile. But where was she going? Rachel took a breath. "I was going to my mother's, but she's not there and I don't know when she'll be back." That was partly true. She didn't have to tell him anything more.

Zoe inadvertently grabbed a chunk of her hair and gave it a good yank. "Ouch." Rachel held on to Zoe's hand so she didn't pull any harder. "My mother didn't know I was coming. I was going to surprise her." Also true.

"Uh-huh." Chewing on his bottom lip, Jake averted his gaze, looked one way, then the other. "I take it you don't you have a key, either."

It was obvious he was thinking she was a real airhead. "You probably didn't hear that she moved. And somehow, I didn't think to get another one."

"Any place else you might want to go? Someplace you can wait until she comes back?"

Rachel finished loosening Zoe's fingers and said, "I've been gone a long time. I haven't kept in contact with anyone." Truth was, she'd never had any good friends here. Being perfect had its draw-backs.

He scratched his chin, stuck one hand in his jacket pocket. "Okay, then. We can go into town and I'll round up a tire someplace and fix it for you. I'll also need a winch to get you out of the ditch."

She did a double-take. His generosity made her feel petty and shallow.

"I'm grateful for your help." Except she didn't have money for a new tire and she was counting on Rick to give her credit because he knew her. Zoe wiggled, then started crying.

Jake opened the door and helped them out. She grabbed the diaper bag and the thermal case with Zoe's food, but he reached around and took them from her.

Zoe cried a little louder. "I'm sorry. She must be hungry or something." More likely Zoe was damned tired of riding in the car going nowhere. And so was she.

"I need to get her carrier, too."

"Where is it?"

"In the back."

Loaded down with baby gear, Jake walked them to his truck. He looked so natural carrying all her stuff, it made her wonder if he'd been around children a lot. She'd heard he wasn't married, but that didn't mean he didn't have kids.

Zoe wailed even louder while Jake stashed the thermal bag behind the front seat. There was only one seat belt that Rachel could see. He put the carrier in the back, then helped her up, practically lifting her into the front seat. There wasn't much she could do except hold Zoe.

"There isn't an air bag on this side is there?" Rachel asked.

"It's an old truck. It doesn't have air bags."

Right. She clipped the seat belt around both of them. "I shouldn't be doing this. It's not safe."

"You can stay here if you want, and I'll do what I can."

Not the best option in her mind. Just

then she got a whiff of a poopy diaper and Zoe let out another wail.

"Shhh," she whispered. "It's okay, sweetie. I'll change you real soon." Geez, she'd just changed her. She shouldn't have given her the juice. She made silly faces at Zoe to distract her.

"I have a better idea," Jake said, scowling. He started the truck, but instead of driving toward town he turned and went the opposite way.

"Where are you going?"

"I'm taking you to my place. It's closer. You can take care of your daughter while I find a tire and someone to get your van out of the ditch."

Zoe stopped wailing, probably because they were moving, but was still sniffling. Rachel brushed the tears from her daughter's chubby cheeks with her thumb. And for some reason, tears began to well in her own eyes. She bit her lip, forcing them away.

It had been a long, trying day, that's all. And Jake's willingness to help her…was more than she'd ever expected. She fought for control, but her voice was still shaky when she said, "I don't know how to thank y—"

"Don't bother," he said, his voice a low rumble. "I'd do it for anyone."

She clamped her mouth shut, her face suddenly burning. She nuzzled Zoe's neck, playing with her so he couldn't see how mortified and angry she felt. She needed his help, and if she didn't have to thank him for it, that was fine with her.

Within minutes they arrived at the Wild Card and he let her inside his apartment through a back door.

"Keep the phone with you," he said, then waved a hand to one side of the room. "There's the bathroom—" and then the other "—and the kitchen." On his way out, he added, "It's not the Ritz."

Zoe had quieted and Rachel stood for a moment staring at the door he'd shut behind him. She wasn't sure his help was worth the humiliation.

Zoe whined and wiggled in Rachel's arm. "Sorry, sweetie. I'll find a spot to change you."

She saw two doorways—one looked as if it went into the bar. The other had a sheet hanging over it. She moved the sheet aside and discovered it was a bedroom.

She flipped a light switch and an old iron lamp on a small gate-leg table next to the bed illuminated the room. The bed looked relatively new, as did the tan comforter. She went over and touched the faux suede. Masculine. Like Jake. One-hundred percent alpha male.

A plump duffel bag and boots lay in one corner, and a small closet without a door revealed some shirts on hangers and a few pairs of jeans.

It was obvious he wasn't staying long.

She gathered what she needed from her bag, then placed Zoe on top of a rubber mat. Zoe gurgled while Rachel placed her fingers in the child's palms, hoping that one day, Zoe would be able to grab hold of them. Her daughter's slightly curly hair was thick and a lighter blond than Rachel's. More like Rachel's had been when she was a child.

She caught Zoe's hand right before she snagged a handful of hair, then leaned down to blow on Zoe's soft little belly. Zoe giggled and squealed, and Rachel couldn't help laughing herself. All Rachel's problems disappeared, however briefly, when she played with Zoe. Early on Rachel had been advised of all the problems she might encounter with her daughter, but no one had told her about the pleasures and rewards.

Back in the kitchen with Zoe saddled on her hip, Rachel opened the small fridge—empty except for some beer and salsa and leftover buffalo wings. If the state of Jake's refrigerator was any indication, he wasn't in any better position than she was.

Maybe he was selling the Wild Card because he needed the money. If that was the case, it didn't make sense that he'd been riding what looked like a brand-new Harley the other day.

After washing her hands, she gave Zoe some juice, then they played and Zoe giggled and gurgled sounds that Rachel imagined were the child's version of "Mama." She kissed Zoe's baby-smooth cheeks and lay beside her, wondering, as she so frequently did, who would protect her girl if she couldn't. How could Alex not want her? How could anyone think she was less than perfect?

Zoe quickly fell asleep, so Rachel buffered her with rolled blankets and pillows, set one of the small baby monitors near her, then stuck the other in her pocket. Back in the kitchen, she paced, looking out the window again and again for Jake's return. She needed a plan. But it was Sunday, and tomorrow night was New Year's Eve and then New Year's Day. It wasn't likely she was going to find any kind of job in the next couple of days.

She walked to the other door that she

knew led to the bar, peered around the corner and switched on the light. A hallway divided the bar from Jake's place. On her left was a door, presumably leading outside. On her right, a stairway going to the second floor. Some of the steps looked as if they had been replaced, in better condition than the rest of the building.

Curious, she started up, testing each step as she went. At the top, she found another switch and flipped it on.

A large chandelier with several bulbs missing hung in the middle of an open room that reminded her of some of the lofts she'd decorated in Chicago. Straight ahead about twenty-five or thirty feet were two big picture windows and, while she couldn't see outside because it was dark, she knew the windows faced the river. Wow. What she could do with this place.

Just then she heard a car. Oh, Lord. Jake would think she was snooping. On her way down the stairs, she smiled. She *was* snooping.

As she reached the bottom step, she heard a knock. Jake wouldn't knock, so she didn't know if she should answer. As soon as she thought it, she realized how ridiculous it was. This was River Bluff, not Chicago.

She went to the bedroom and peeked in on Zoe who was still asleep. Another knock. Louder.

"Who's there?" she asked at the door.

"I'm looking for Jake Chandler. My name is Mike Dempsey."

Dempsey wasn't a name she knew. "He's—busy."

Thinking she heard him swear, she waited for him to say something else, and when he didn't, she added, "Come back later."

"I'd rather not. I drove from San Antonio and I'm here to talk to him about his property."

She opened the door a crack.

A tall man in a dark suit smiled reassuringly.

Odd. Jake had been going somewhere

when he'd found Rachel in the ditch. If he'd been expecting someone, he would've stuck around, wouldn't he? "Like I said, I'll tell him you were here."

"Would you please have him call me?" He held out a card. "It's important."

As the man began walking away, Rachel saw headlights coming down the driveway. Within seconds, Jake pulled in, sprang out of the truck like a missile and slammed the door.

He stalked over to Dempsey. "Don't you have a calendar?"

She closed the door, but not all the way. She could still see Jake and the other man standing under the outside light.

"Or maybe you don't understand English."

"My client is anxious to get the deal done—whatever it takes."

She saw Jake clench his hands. "Well, tell your client I'm thinking I like it here and I'm getting the urge to renovate the place, instead. In fact, right now I'm leaning more than ninety percent that way." Jake turned for the saloon.

"But—" Dempsey sputtered. "It's a new offer. I guarantee you'll change your mind. And if you don't like it, we'll talk."

Jake froze. "We still have an appointment next Tuesday. I suggest you come back then."

Rachel wished she could see the other guy's face. She admired Jake's ability to hold his ground. He never had seemed to give a damn whether someone liked him or not. She'd been just the opposite, caring too much about what other people thought. She'd learned the hard way that no one respected you if you didn't respect yourself.

"Uh—okay. Sure thing," Dempsey said. He gave Jake a thumbs-up. "See you Tuesday, then. Have fun."

Jake didn't come in right away, but when he did, he was carrying a big bag. The scent of barbecue sauce filled the air. She immediately started salivating. He set the bag on the table.

"Help yourself."

She wanted to tear into it, but held back, maintaining some semblance of the class she used to have. "What is it?"

"Ribs from the café."

"Yum. I love Eddie's ribs. And I'm starving."

One side of his mouth tipped up in what looked suspiciously like a smile. But just as quickly it was gone. "Then you'd better eat. Napkins and utensils are in the bag. You can find something to drink in the fridge."

"What about you?"

"I've got to get some things from the shed. Someone's coming to help me get your truck out of the ditch."

"But you should eat, too."

He gave her a funny look. "I will." He was still looking at her a little strangely as he went outside.

She stared at the sack of food, hungry enough to eat the bag and all. Then she heard Zoe. She went back to the bedroom and brought Zoe out to the kitchen. With Zoe on her hip, she pulled the box of ribs out of the bag, followed by coleslaw, hot biscuits, napkins, plastic plates and utensils, and made two place settings. Debating whether to wait for Jake or not, her stomach decided for her.

"Zoe," she said, "you're so going to wish you had teeth. Eddie's ribs are amazing."

Her stomach growled again. She placed Zoe in her seat and brought her to sit near the table. After winding up a musical toy and setting it next to Zoe, she sat, picked up a rib and bit into it. Oh, man. She closed her eyes and, with the meat still between her teeth, savored the tangy flavor. If food could cause an orgasm, Eddie's ribs would do it.

She heard a chair scrape against the wood floor, opened her eyes and saw Jake lowering himself next to her. "Meditating?"

She put the bone down, licking the sauce from her lips. "The scent alone puts me in a trance." She smiled. "But you know how good they are."

He motioned to Zoe who was sucking on her fist. "What's the kid's name?"

"The kid is a girl, not a goat, and her name is Zoe."

"Zoe. Can she eat this stuff?"

Rachel laughed. "Nope."

"She looks like she wants something."

"She's teething. She'll chew on anything, but not ribs."

He picked up a section with his fork, cut off a hunk and started eating.

"Thanks for doing this. I was starving. But—I'll have to pay you back later. I don't have any cash with me."

"Forget it."

"I can't pay to get my tire fixed, either."

Frowning, he stopped eating and looked at her. "And your mother isn't home."

She nodded.

"What's going on with you, Rachel?"

Her heart sank. "What difference does it make?"

He stared for a moment, then stabbed another piece of meat with his fork. The angry thrust made her wince.

"It doesn't. I'll get your vehicle fixed. You don't have to repay me."

Words caught in her throat. The man who hated her was going to help her…and he wanted to pay for it.

"Where's your husband?"

She swallowed, then said softly, "I'm divorced. I have no idea where he is."

He glanced at Zoe. "And the baby—doesn't he see her?"

She looked down and shook her head. She couldn't get into her personal life with Jake.

"He's a scumbag."

Her gaze met his. "Excuse me?"

"Any guy who doesn't see his own kid is a scumbag."

"Well—" she laughed wryly "—that's one thing we agree on."

Abruptly, Jake pushed his chair back and stood. Rachel stopped laughing, uncertain what she'd said wrong. He went to a cupboard, got out two glasses and filled them with water. She watched as he put them down hard on the table and sat again. "Does he do anything for her?"

Rachel shook her head. "He didn't want kids," she said slowly. "So when I became pregnant—and then we heard Zoe would have special needs—well…" Her heart beat faster. "It didn't work out, that's all," she finished almost inaudibly.

He looked uncomfortable. No, he looked like he wanted to bolt.

"Zoe has Down syndrome," she said, quickly pulling herself together and relieving him of the need to ask. "I couldn't help overhearing you tell that man you might renovate instead of selling the place. If you do, I hope you'll consider hiring me."

He kept eating.

"I really am good at what I do. I have

references and a portfolio somewhere in the van. This place has so much potential. You ought to think about it. Especially since I can get supplies at dealers costs, and—"

Lights flashed outside and she heard a car drive up.

Jake launched to his feet. "That's Brady."

"Brady Carrick? I heard he was playing professional football."

"He was." He shrugged into his denim jacket. "Be ready when I get back."

Jake refused to talk about his friends with Rachel. Eating dinner with her and talking about her baby were hard enough. Jake had to remember, she was just a woman who wanted a job. Not his concern. Though he did feel for the kid.

He could tell something else was going on with Rachel, but that wasn't his concern, either.

She tugged on his sleeve, stopping him.

"I *need* a job, Jake. If you renovate, I'd

be truly grateful if you'd give me a chance."

He thought he saw her bottom lip quiver. "Please," she said. "At least put my name on your list."

He could hear the desperation in her voice. See it in her eyes. She dropped her hand.

"*If* I decide to renovate, I'll consider it."

Even before the door slammed behind him, he wanted to bite his tongue. He couldn't hire her. He couldn't do business with someone as devious as she was.

# CHAPTER FIVE

"SORRY, IT TOOK SO LONG to get this sucker out," Jake said, standing with Brady beside the idling VW bus they'd just dragged out of the ditch. After giving it a jump, Jake wasn't sure it would start again if he shut off the engine. "I appreciate your help."

"No problem." Brady glanced at his watch. "I'll make it."

"Hot date tonight?"

"Not so hot. I'm working. Doing some research," Brady answered.

Jake laughed. "Yeah? Stefi says your work is a blonde in Bandera."

"Stefi's got a big mouth. And I seem to remember seeing you—"

"Ah-ah-ah." Jake raised a hand.

"Remember you're talkin' to someone who knows your deepest, darkest secrets," Jake kidded. "Like what happened after the homecoming ga—"

"Okay!" Brady held up both hands. "You blackhearted S.O.B. But you'd better remember blackmail goes both ways." He started toward his truck.

"Maybe you should bring her along tomorrow night? Make our New Year's Eve party a little more interesting," Jake called after his buddy.

Brady turned. "Sure. I'll bring her and you bring Rachel." He gave Jake an *I-gotcha* grin.

I gotcha was right. Jake felt his stomach seize as he thought of Rachel waiting at his place. He climbed into the driver's seat of her VW and saw the red oil light. The gas tank was nearly empty and she needed a new tire.

He'd brought along the spare to his pickup because he needed something on the van to get it out of the ditch. But it would have to be replaced with a tire that fit. On a Saturday night in River Bluff, the chances of finding one would be slim. And Sunday morning in the Bible belt would be even worse.

He was about to pull out his cell to call Stefi and tell her he wouldn't make it, then remembered he'd left it with Rachel. *Rachel Diamonte*.

As he drove toward town, memories flashed through his head. The night he'd found Rachel at the river stranded after her date dumped her. He'd taken her home on his beat-up Harley. The night he'd seen her with Kyle Barstow. *The night of the fire*.

He hadn't thought about it in years. And he didn't want to now. Ten minutes later, he stopped at the Gas 'n Go station in River Bluff, hoping the owner, Art Swanson, just might have an old tire stashed somewhere. But instead, he found a note on the door saying Art was at the hardware store with Harry watching a football game.

Jake couldn't think what football

game, since the Super Bowl was a few weeks away. But he went to the payphone in front of the station and called the hardware store, anyway. Later, when Art showed up all disgruntled, Jake wasn't surprised. Art had always been grumpy.

After getting gas and oil, Jake helped Art search the garage for a tire. While they were looking, Jake noticed a teenager in a tricked-out GTO pull in, get gas and then come inside to pay.

While the kid was looking at the snacks on a rack, Art said to Jake, "The tread on that spare is about shot."

"That's why I need a tire, Art."

"Well, can't help you now. You can leave the vehicle here and I'll call around for a tire tomorrow."

"But then I'll need a ride home."

"I'm going out that way," the kid, who was obviously listening, piped up. "I can give you a ride, Mr. Chandler."

Jake didn't recognize him. He looked sixteen at the most, too young to have been around before Jake left town. "That's real nice of you," Jake said. "How come you know me and I don't know you?"

The teen blushed. "Everyone knows you're back in town, Mr. Chandler."

Yeah, that's what he was afraid of. "What's your name?"

"Wyatt."

Jake smiled. "Good to meet you, Wyatt."

"So, what do you say?" Art prodded. "You gonna go with Wyatt? I want to get back to the game."

"No, thanks. I'll drive back and call you tomorrow to see what you come up with." Jake turned to the boy. "Thanks anyway for the offer." Motioning to the phone on the counter, Jake asked Art, "Do you mind?"

"Help yourself. Just make it quick so I can get back."

"Sure." Jake reached in his pocket and pulled out Stefi's cell number and dialed. "It's Jake," he said when she answered.

"It's about time. Where the hell are you?"

"Something came up. I'm not going to make it."

Stefi was silent, so he added, "I'll have to take a rain check." That seemed to appease her.

The kid followed Jake outside. "I used to go fishing near your place with my dad."

"Good fishing in that part of the river."

"My dad said you were a great football player when you went to school here."

Jake laughed. "I think your dad's confused. Brady Carrick was the star player."

"Yeah, but I heard you were one of the best until you got—" His voice trailed off as if realizing he'd said the wrong thing.

"Before I got busted," Jake finished the sentence.

Wyatt chewed on his bottom lip, his fingers tapping nervously on his thigh. "Is—it true?"

"Is what true?" Jake said, knowing damned well what the kid wanted to know. But he was going to have to work for it.

"Well, uh, you know. The fire and the horses. Did you get arrested?"

Jake stopped in his tracks, his blood pumping. "No, I didn't. One thing you better learn if you plan to stick around this town, Wyatt. People have to have someone to blame when things go wrong."

The teen looked as if he understood…until he frowned and said, "But if it isn't true, why not say so? You can't let people think the worst if it's not true."

Jake scoffed. "It's history. It's not important anymore." The important thing was that he got the hell out of River Bluff when he did.

"So everything they say is just made up?"

"*Everything* covers a lot of territory. *Everything* is what people want to believe it is. I'd guess maybe half of what people say is true." And he wasn't going to explain which half. "What's your dad's name?"

The teen shoved a rock with the toe of his boot. "My dad moved away. My parents are divorced."

"Ah," Jake said, understanding a little where all the questions were coming from. The guy related to Jake's circumstances. "That's tough."

"I can handle it."

The bravado in the kid's voice was familiar—much the same as Jake had sounded when he was about that age. "Good. You gotta let some stuff just roll off your back."

Jake reached out to shake hands. "Well, maybe we'll bump into each other again."

Wyatt smiled and then watched as Jake got into the van and drove off. When Jake reached the Wild Card, he stood for a moment in the drive. It was past nine, the lights were on inside the apartment, and for just a fraction of a second, he remembered what it was like when he'd come home after school to find his mom waiting for him. She'd been his biggest champion.

He went inside, careful not to make noise. Everything was quiet and it looked as if no one was there. Except for the light.

He pulled aside the curtain covering the doorway to the bedroom to see Rachel and the baby fast asleep. Rachel had buffered Zoe with some kind of rolled padding and pillows. They looked peaceful, and considering what Rachel had been through earlier, she was probably exhausted.

Watching the two of them sleep, Rachel's hand over the baby's, there was no mistaking a mother's love for her child. He couldn't imagine how Rachel hooked up with some low-life scum who'd skip out on his own kid.

He let the curtain fall, and then went to get a beer from the fridge. Taking a swig, he walked into the old bar and flicked the light switch. A bulb flashed and popped, but one lone light lit up the far end of the room. Chairs had been turned upside down on top of a table, and the legs cast long shadows down the cracked plaster walls, like bars on a jail cell.

His gaze drifted to a faded poster of Paris and the Eiffel Tower that still clung to one of the walls, its edges curled and torn. He remembered the very day his mother had hung it. She'd laughed and said it was a reminder that one day, when the Wild Card prospered, she was going to go to Paris and stroll down the Champs Elysées.

She never did. She'd never gone anywhere. His mother had a dream and she'd worked like a dog to make it come true. But it never happened. Hell, if Wade Barstow was in fact Jake's father, why hadn't he stepped up and helped his mom get ahead? He had money… But Jake didn't know if Wade was his dad. When he'd pressed his mother for his father's name, she'd said George Smith. At ten years old, that didn't mean much. When Jake got older, he realized how common the name was and that his mother had probably given it to him to appease him. Make sure he'd never bother Barstow. He'd probably never know the truth unless he could get a DNA test. But that would never happen.

If it was true, then Barstow was a man who took no responsibility for his actions. A man with no conscience—and no honor.

In Jake's book, that was worse than anything his so-called unsavory mother had ever done.

RACHEL HEARD ZOE make a snuffling sound. Groggy, she rubbed her eyes. They were at Jake's, she remembered. She glanced at Zoe but the baby was still asleep, restless. Gosh, what time was it? It was still dark outside, but light leaked through the curtain covering the doorway. She thought she'd left the table lamp on....

She rolled gently off the bed so as not to wake Zoe, then stole to the door and pulled back the curtain. A small light was on in the kitchen and it cast enough of a glow to see into the living area where Jake was sprawled on top of the couch, one foot on the floor, one arm across his bare chest, the other raised and covering his eyes. The low lighting played with forms and shapes, making Jake's chest muscles stand out in bas-relief.

Seeing him like that made her pulse race. She couldn't deny that she'd always been infatuated with Jake. Or maybe back then she liked the idea of feeling something no one expected of her.

She checked her watch—6:00 a.m. Zoe would be waking soon for breakfast and then they'd have to leave. If he'd had any luck with the van. Maybe that's why he hadn't woken her.

She went to the window. Didn't see the VW anywhere, though he could've parked on the other side of the saloon.

As she went back into the kitchen, she thought about how accommodating Jake had been. He could've left her in the ditch.

As she stood at the sink, she heard a noise, swung around and bumped into Jake. Her hand landed on his chest. "Oh," she said, pulling it back. "You scared me."

"Sorry." He shrugged.

She ducked around him and walked to the table. "Why didn't you wake me when you got back?"

As he emptied the coffee pot and made a fresh brew, he said quietly, "I couldn't get a tire and I didn't think you'd want to drive an unsafe vehicle in the dark."

Within moments, the aroma of coffee filled the kitchen. She worried her fingers over her mouth. "Did you bring the van back here?"

He nodded, sitting at the table beside her. "It's out back."

"I'm sorry I put you through all this.

I'm sure you had better ways to spend a Saturday night."

He looked at her with sleepy eyes. His dark hair was messy and she tried to keep from looking at his half-naked body.

"This is River Bluff. Unless I'm playing poker, this is about as exciting as it gets."

She smiled. "I remember you guys always getting in trouble for playing poker—gambling—in high school. The Wild Bunch."

He smiled. "Cole's sister, Annie, started that. I suppose the label fit." Then as if he'd realized he'd been too friendly, too familiar, he got up and pulled on a long-sleeved black shirt hanging over the back of the couch. Then he went back to the counter and picked up the coffee pot. "Would you like some?"

She nodded. "Yes, please."

"Hope you like it black. I'm not stocked for company."

"Black is fine, and I'm not exactly company."

After handing her a cup, he took his

and went to the window where he pulled the curtain back. She could see a glow of sunlight just breaking the horizon beyond the river. "I'm sorry about your uncle," she said.

Still gazing outside, he said, "Thanks. We weren't that close."

"Do you mind if I feed Zoe breakfast before we go?"

He turned to face her. "The van isn't safe to drive. I don't know how you made it this far."

"You mean there's something other than the tire?"

"It is the tire. I couldn't get yours replaced and the one I put on isn't safe. When you're ready, I can take you to your mother's or you can make your own arrangements. Your choice."

Her choice. She had money enough for a night, maybe even two, if she didn't eat, at the motel.

"Before I go, can I show you my work? As I said before, I have my portfolio in the van."

Jake didn't like the plea in her eyes. If he looked at her work, she'd probably think he was interested. But if he did decide to renovate… "Okay. Can't hurt to look."

Her face broke into a giant smile and her eyes lit up. "I'll be right back," she said quickly, then hurried out the door.

Jake heard a sharp wail from the bedroom. He went to the door and saw the baby near the edge of the bed. In one quick step he was beside her and had scooped her into his arms.

He hadn't held many babies, but for some reason, it felt perfectly natural. Zoe's face puckered. "Hey," he said in a soft voice, "it's okay. Your mommy will be right back." He bounced her gently in his arms and when she smiled, he felt like some kind of magician. "You're a pretty cool, kid, aren't you?"

The baby turned, her arm hitting his nose, and he turned and saw Rachel standing in the doorway. "She started to cry," he said. "And it looked like she was going to fall off the bed."

"Hey, punkin. Did you sleep well?" Taking the baby from him, she said, "My portfolio is on the table if you want to look at it while I change Zoe and feed her."

Jake watched Rachel go to the bedroom before he opened the book. It was filled with sketches and photographs of home interiors, some offices and a couple of restaurants. Having used a designer for his offices in San Diego, he recognized various types of décor, from ultramodern to old-world elegance. He was surprised to see some edgier pop-culture concepts as well. Each project was unique, displaying Rachel's skillful use of colors and themes appropriate to the venue.

She'd been a perfectionist in school, and that trait seemed to work well for her in her career. She had a strong ability to create diverse looks, even styles he couldn't imagine the straight-laced Rachel he knew in high school relating to at all. But then, there were a lot of years in between and who knows what kind of life she'd been living.

If her car was any example, she hadn't been living the high life. But that didn't make sense, either. She'd had a business in Chicago and from her work, a thriving one.

He glanced up to see her putting Zoe into her seat. When she was finished she brought the baby over and set her on the floor next to the table. "Do you mind if I warm her food in the microwave?"

"Use whatever you need to," he said, then noticed Zoe looking up at him. "Hey, kiddo. What's up?" The baby blew a spit bubble, then made a bunch of noises ending in "Yahyahyah."

"She thinks she's carrying on a conversation," Rachel said from the kitchen. "If she gets encouragement, she'll go on forever."

"Is that right," he said, looking at Zoe.

"Yahyahyah." Zoe made a high-pitched squeal.

Rachel brought over a couple of bottles of baby food and a plastic cup with a spout. "I'm surprised she's not afraid of you. She's been going through a clingy stage. I suppose being uprooted might be the cause."

"Maybe she's homesick?"

"I don't know that a baby can be homesick, but I'm sure she knows she's in unfamiliar surroundings."

He felt awkward, as if he should be doing something, but he didn't know what. He was hungry, but he had little in the way of food, just some bread and a few eggs. Rachel would probably get breakfast at her mother's when she got there, but he couldn't make something for himself and not ask.

"Since you can't drive the van, I'll take you to your mother's when you're done," he said. "Art at the Gas 'n Go was going to check for a tire when he got the chance, so you can call him about getting it fixed."

She looked at him, then went back to feeding Zoe. "Okay. I'll call Art later."

Well, that settled that. "I'm making myself eggs and toast and can make extra if you'd like." Then he quickly added, "But I imagine your mother will have something better when you get there."

She turned his way, but didn't meet his gaze. He had the distinct feeling something was wrong and it had to do with her mother. But that didn't make sense.

"Uh—actually, I'm starving right now and I'd love an egg."

"Okay, I'll make enough for two." He was right. But whatever was going on, it wasn't any of his business. He went to the fridge, found the eggs and bread and placed them on the metal table next to the stove that doubled as a counter. Since he hadn't planned to stay in River Bluff, his kitchen supplies were sparse.

"I'm making one-eyed gypsies," he said.

She glanced up.

"I don't have a toaster, so I melt a little

butter in a frying pan, fry the bread on one side, turn it over and make a hole in the middle for the eggs."

"Yum. It sounds delicious." Rachel's eyes brightened as she leaned back in her chair.

"It's a camper's trick," he said, as he tossed some butter into the oversize frying pan and turned on the burner.

"That's probably why I never heard of it. I never had the camping experience. My mother hated doing things like that."

Not a surprise. Sarah Diamonte wouldn't want to get her delicate hands dirty. "Would you have gone if she'd wanted you to?" He placed four slices of bread in the sizzling butter.

"Maybe. But I was too busy studying. Too busy being perfect."

She didn't disguise her anger. "Well, you'll have to make sure little Zoe has the opportunity when she gets older." Zoe smiled as if she'd understood he was talking about her, then made more kid noises.

"I plan to do a lot of things with her," Rachel said.

Jake got the feeling that she meant a lot of things Rachel hadn't been able to do.

He flipped over each piece of bread, then took a spoon and made a hole in the middle of each slice.

"So—" she said, then hesitated, picking at something on the sleeve of her sweater. "So—what did you think about my work?"

He cracked the eggs, one into each slice. "It's good. You're a talented designer."

She sat up a little taller. "Really? Did you like it enough to consider hiring me?" She smiled, then said quickly, "I mean if you were to decide to renovate."

She was persistent, he had to give her that. Somehow it made her more likeable. He'd always thought she was the kind of person who'd had everything dropped into her lap.

"I'm curious, though. Your work is

outstanding, and the photographs indicate you had a lot of business in Chicago. Why leave if your business was thriving?"

Her smile shut down like a power outage. A furrow formed between her brows. "My business depended on my husband's referrals—and his money for advertising. Once we divorced, the referrals and the money disappeared."

"Well, your work speaks for itself."

"You'd think." She shook her head. "It's complicated. And not important anymore. I'm here and I need work."

What she meant was that it wasn't any of his business. And she was right.

"If my work speaks for itself," she said, "does that mean you'll give me a chance? I mean, if you decide to go ahead?"

He clenched his teeth. "*If*—" he said "—and that's a humongous if—*if* I decide to renovate."

Her smile spread from one side of her face to the other.

He had a hard time pulling his gaze from hers. Until he smelled something burning. He grabbed the metal frying pan handle, searing his fingers as he dumped it on the side table with a clang, causing Zoe to shriek. "Breakfast is ready," he said, his words sharp. He ran cold water on his hand.

He needed to pay attention to what he was doing. Not get caught up in someone else's problems.

Rachel picked Zoe up and instantly the baby was quiet. He'd said he'd give her a shot. Rachel tried to quell her excitement. *If* he was going to renovate. Yet, somehow, her intuition said he was going to do it. If not, he'd have left the Wild Card in the hands of a real-estate agent and been long gone by now. It was obvious to her that Jake had unfinished business in River Bluff, even if he didn't know it.

He set two eggs in front of her. "It looks wonderful," she said. "Smells wonderful, too." She placed Zoe back in her seat.

"I don't suppose she can eat any of this."

"No. Like most children with the condition, she has difficulties with eating. But she's doing so well, I don't think it will be long before she can."

He sat in the chair next to her, handed her a fork. "I've got some things to do in a little while, so I can give you a ride to your mother's if you want."

"That's—nice of you. I do appreciate all you've done, especially since—" She couldn't finish. "Well, you know. I'm very grateful."

A scowl suddenly appeared on his face.

"It might be easier if I waited to talk to Art," she suggested timidly. "If he finds a tire and brings it out, I can drive the van and wouldn't have to come back for it."

He was silent while they finished eating. Then, standing, he picked up the dishes, took them to the sink and ran some water. "Whatever you want." He shrugged. "After I shower, I've got to go. If Art comes, you can lock up behind you."

Fine with her. It would give her time to make a plan.

When he started washing the dishes, she said, "Let me do that."

He stopped instantly, wiped his hands and left the room. If she didn't know better, she might think he was trying to get away from her.

After finishing the dishes, she picked up Jake's cell phone to call the Trail's End Motel. She might as well get a room and work out the other stuff later.

"Okay, I'm outta here." Jake's deep voice preceded him as he came from the bedroom.

He smelled like fresh soap and his hair was still damp and looped a little over his forehead.

She handed him the cell phone. "Sorry. I was just going to make a quick call."

He waved it away. "No, you keep it

until you leave. You shouldn't be without a phone. I won't be back until late, so be sure to lock up when you go."

"I will." As he reached the door, she couldn't help asking, "Jake—have you ever thought about renting out the upstairs?"

He stopped. "No. And—"

"I'd like to rent it," she said before he could elaborate. "If you sell the place, I'll just move. And if you decide to renovate, maybe we could work out a deal. My work in exchange for some of the rent?"

His incredulous expression told her he thought she was a wacko. He shook his head and practically sprinted out the door.

"I really appreciate all you've done," she called after him, but he gave no acknowledgment that he'd heard her.

## CHAPTER SIX

THE WOMAN WAS RELENTLESS, Jake decided as he pulled into a parking spot in front of the Longhorn Café. He'd already had breakfast, but he had to find a place to regroup and make some decisions.

At some point, he had to go to San Antonio to get his Uncle Verne's car out of hock, and he could also check for a tire if Art hadn't already done it.

Getting out, he saw a couple of vehicles he recognized and a couple he didn't. The black King Ranch Ford belonged to Hank Chisum, Luke's older brother. Over the years, Luke and Hank had had plenty of differences, Jake knew, but he'd thought they'd got past them when Luke went to Iraq. But from what Luke had told him, the strain between the brothers was even greater.

Entering the café, the aroma of bacon and homemade cinnamon rolls made him hungry all over again. He glanced around, then saw Stefi in a corner booth. She waved him over.

On his way, he nodded to Sally and Harold Knutson. Harold had been the one to tell Jake that Luke's brother sat in on an occasional poker game, but so far, they hadn't been at any together. Jake said, "Mornin'," to Hank on his way by.

"Hey, Stef," he greeted as he reached her booth.

"Sit with me," she said.

Just then Jake's blood rushed as he recognized the man sitting in the booth behind Stefi, his back to Jake. It took all his willpower to rein himself in. "No thanks," he said succinctly. "I'm getting coffee to go."

The silver-haired man turned, looked directly at Jake and nodded.

Ignoring the acknowledgment, Jake went to the counter. He heard Stefi say after him, "Geez, what got into you this morning?"

His nerves on fire, Jake ordered coffee to go. It wasn't until after he ordered that he saw the kid he'd met at the gas station yesterday sitting on the stool next to him.

"Hi, Mr. Chandler."

Jake nodded. "Wyatt."

"Is it true you might be staying?" Wyatt asked, then looked toward Barstow's booth. "To open the Wild Card again? I heard it was a pretty lively place back in the day."

Before he could answer, Jake felt the warmth of a body beside him and turned to see Stefi.

"What're you doing tomorrow night?" she asked in a breathy drawl. "I was thinking of having a New Year's Eve party."

Jake knew what kind of party she had in mind and it consisted of two people, her and him. As attractive as she was, he'd never been attracted—not in the way she had in mind, anyway. "Sorry, sweetheart. I already have plans."

Stefi frowned. "Your loss," she said, then went back to her booth where her food was getting cold. Interestingly, Hank soon proceeded to her table and sat across from her.

"Here you are, Mr. Chandler," Jennifer said, placing one coffee to go in front of him and eyeing Wyatt as if he was a box of chocolates.

"I'd like one of those cinnamon rolls, too, Jennifer." If he knew whether Rachel would still be at his place when he got back, he'd order a half-dozen. Her kid could probably eat gooey bread dough.

He'd been equally surprised and shocked when Rachel had asked to rent the upstairs of the Wild Card in exchange for work. Why ask him for work when she could simply go to her mother's?

There was no love lost between Jake and Sarah Diamonte. The woman had carried a vendetta against the Wild Card from the moment she'd found her husband passed out on a couch in Jake's mother's living room. And Jake, asleep in the bedroom at the time, had been awakened by the woman's vitriolic diatribe against his mother. He'd run out and kicked her in the shin, shouting at her to stay away from his mother or she'd be sorry.

He'd only been seven at the time.

He wondered if Rachel even knew how much her mother had hated his mother. Made so many other women in the community hate her, too. When his mother had gotten sick, she'd had no will to fight the gossip and innuendo. Not even for her son.

"Yo, Jake," a male voice blared.

Jake looked up. Ed Falconetti in his white cook's apron peered through the opening to the kitchen. "Hey, Big Ed. What's up?" A New Jersey native,

Eddie's Texas drawl had an east-coast accent. Upon meeting him, people often thought he'd come from a foreign country.

"The charity benefit at the high school tomorrow. And poker on Wednesday. You'll be there, right?"

"Yes on the poker. But I'm going to San Antonio tonight, so I don't know about the benefit." The town, in conjunction with Mike Bailey, the editor and publisher of the River's Run, still had a New Year's Day benefit to help kids going through cancer treatment.

"Yes, you do." Jake turned and saw Blake coming in the door.

The older man sat on the stool next to him, then slapped a hand on the counter. "It's the most attended event in River Bluff. The entire who's who of Southern Texas will be there."

"I know." Jake avoided looking at the booth where Barstow sat. That's why he didn't want to be there. Though Jake had been back four weeks and Barstow's attorney was making offers on the Wild Card for him, this was the only time he'd actually seen his rumored "father." And that was exactly how Jake wanted it. But he'd look like Scrooge if he didn't go.

Jennifer brought Jake's cinnamon roll.

"I'll have some of those to go," Blake said. "Annie's craving them."

"Oh, man," Eddie said. "You know a guy is happily married when he drives thirty miles for cinnamon rolls."

"Congratulations again." Jake looked at Blake, but his mind quickly went to other things. "Luke says you've got some contacts with contractors in San Antonio."

"I do. I'd be happy to hook you up with a few if you want. They'll give you a deal."

"It's just a question."

"Uh-huh," Blake said. "Well, let me know when it becomes a reality. I'll be glad to help. We could have an old-fashioned barn raising."

Dammit. Jake didn't want to make it sound as if he was actually going ahead with it, but he wanted Barstow to know he wasn't that easy to get rid of.

"Make that a bar raising," Eddie chimed in. "I can pound a nail with the best of them. We could have that sucker up in no time."

Jake heard the door slam behind him and turning, he saw Barstow leave. A knot formed in his stomach. He took a deep breath and, smiling, he said to Blake and Ed, "I'm looking at sale offers this week. If any of you want to get in on the action, let me know."

And that's when he decided, he was going to have to confront Barstow. If Barstow wasn't Jake's father, then who was?

WITH ZOE IN HER ARMS, Rachel walked from the riverbank toward the pecan grove. Art was working on a tire and would call her back. Jake was gone until this evening, so she'd taken advantage of the opportunity to look around the place to get ideas.

The pecan grove had a clearing in the middle that could easily be used for an outdoor concert area and for dancing. All they had to do was build a raised stage and put in a portable dance floor. With the right lighting, the area could be ideal for weddings and receptions as well.

Just thinking about the possibilities excited her. Taking the germ of an idea and making it come full circle was the most fun. She usually brainstormed with her customers, but not before doing a thorough job of brainstorming on her own. Any and all ideas were fair game.

She glanced around, remembering how the grove had been popular for making out way back when. She wondered if the current crop of teens also used it. Seeing no empty cans or cigarette butts, no recent tire tracks, she decided not.

She felt an ache of nostalgia. The grove held both good and bad memories for her. The worst and the best. Kyle Barstow had left her stranded here when she wouldn't give him what he wanted. That same night, Jake had come to her rescue and had given her a ride home on his motor-cycle.

She'd never forgotten what had been the most freeing experience in her life. Even now she could recall the crisp autumn wind against her face, the scent of leather from Jake's jacket, the feel of his young body against hers as she clung to him.

The sound of a car motor brought her alert. It was too early for Jake to return. Quickly, she left the grove and walked toward the Wild Card where she saw a van parked, and two women get out.

As she got closer, she realized one of the women was her mother. Good Lord, what on earth was she doing here? Sarah couldn't have come here for Rachel and Zoe, could she? She didn't know they were here. Or did she?

Rachel felt a tug of emotion. Maybe her mother had learned about the van breaking down from someone in town, and maybe she'd come to get Rachel and Zoe to stay with her.

As Rachel walked closer, her mother finally noticed her, and her expression registered pure shock.

"Rachel? What are you doing here?"

"Hello, Mother. It's nice to see you again."

Sarah's face reddened. "You didn't answer me, Rachel."

"I… My car broke down and Jake was helping me get it fixed. I thought maybe you'd heard and—"

"Mary and I are here for other reasons."

"Oh," Rachel said, taken aback. She hugged Zoe closer. "Why?"

"Things we need to take up with Jake Chandler. Nothing you'd be interested in. Especially since you're not staying in River Bluff."

Rachel didn't recognize the woman called Mary. "I'm Sarah's daughter, Rachel," she said, extending her free hand. "And this is Zoe, her granddaughter."

Sarah tugged on the woman's arm. "We need to speak to the owner of the property," Sarah said to Mary, and then started for the apartment in back.

Though it was chilly outside, Rachel felt as if a furnace had been lit inside her. "He's not here. He won't be back until late tonight. But I'd be happy to give him a message if you'd like to leave one."

Sarah spun around. "It's not a good idea for you to stay here, Rachel. It looks…it's just not good. Even if you're waiting to get your car fixed."

"Oh, well I don't have much choice, do I? Not since you threw me and Zoe out into the street."

Quickly Sarah came over and pulled Rachel away so the other woman couldn't hear her. "I realize you're angry at me because I didn't just up and give you what you wanted. But making a scene in front of my colleague isn't going to change anything."

"Colleague?"

"Yes. We've formed a coalition to keep establishments such as the Wild Card out of our community."

"Oh, I see. And what exactly does this coalition do?"

"Just what I said. We make sure taverns don't take hold in our community."

"But they already have."

"Not for long if we can help it."

Rachel said through clenched jaws, "And what are you planning to do to prevent it?"

"That's not important. What is important is that you leave here now. We'll give you a ride."

"I don't need one."

"Don't be silly."

"I'm serious. I'm going to rent out the upstairs from Jake and start my business."

In the space of a second, Sarah's face went from pink to red to purple. When she finally regained some semblance of poise, she said through her teeth, "Do you know how that will look to people?"

If it wasn't so sad, Rachel might've laughed at the comment. "At this point, all I care about is providing for my daughter."

WADE BARSTOW DROVE DOWN the long road to his home and saw Dempsey's car parked in the circular drive. He hoped the man had made some progress and had at least presented the offer to Chandler. He was tired of people who didn't know how to do their job.

Getting out of his pickup, Wade walked over to the dark sedan. The window went down.

"Hope you've got good news, Mike," Wade said. "I could use some about now."

The lawyer got out, briefcase in hand. They went into the house through the door that led directly to Wade's home office. Wade motioned for Dempsey to sit in one of the chairs near the massive fireplace that dominated the room. He opened a humidor on the coffee table and offered the lawyer a cigar.

Dempsey declined, so he closed the top. "Drink?" Wade walked to the bar on the opposite side.

"No, thanks."

He took a bottle of water from the refrigerator behind the bar and came back to sit across from the lawyer.

"Have you got a signature?" Wade liked to do things quickly. Make a decision, get the job done.

"No signature, no counter. I can't even get the guy to look at it until Tuesday."

"He wants to sell. What's holding things up?"

"He didn't say, but—I have the feeling it's you."

"Me?"

"He asked who the buyer was and wouldn't talk to me until I told him."

Wade smiled. Jake was a smart young man. Wade had gotten a background check on Chandler before they'd even drafted the offer. He'd felt remiss for not watching out for the boy as he'd promised Lola. After the teen left town, he'd lost track of him. Wade had been impressed when he heard how well Jake had done with his dot-com business, a high-tech information network that rivaled the best of them.

But Wade's relationship with the man's mother didn't have anything to do with business decisions. He needed the property. "So you told him?"

Dempsey nodded. "I had to."

Wade stood, impatient with the man's apparent ineptitude. "That's crap. You don't have to do anything."

Mike shrugged. "Okay, but I thought it might make a difference. You're an important man in this community. How could I know he hated you?"

Mike's statement cut. "He said that?"

"No, but I saw his reaction when I told him you were the LLC."

Wade rubbed his chin. Suddenly he felt tired. Old and tired.

"I'm seeing him on Tuesday, so I wanted to discuss what the next step might be if he's not interested. How high do you want to go?"

"Whatever it takes. He doesn't need the money, so find out his price, money or otherwise."

Dempsey stood. "That's what I wanted to know." He picked up his briefcase and headed for the door. "I'll be in touch."

Wade watched the man get into his car, then heard a knock at the inside door.

"Dad? You alone? I need to talk."

"C'mon in, Wyatt."

## CHAPTER SEVEN

JAKE TIGHTENED THE last bolt on the tire.
After hitching a ride to San Antonio with
Art, Jake had gotten his uncle's car out
of hock and picked up the tire at the same
time. He'd hoped Rachel would still be
at his place when he returned, so she
could take her vehicle and kid and leave.

But she wasn't. She'd left his phone
and she'd also forgotten to take a small
baby blanket and her portfolio.

Finished with the tire, he placed the
disposable cell phone he'd purchased
inside Rachel's van on the front seat and
went inside.

He turned on the radio to his favorite
country station, sat at the table, then
flipped open her portfolio again. She'd

said she had ideas for the Wild Card, and if they were as good as the work in front of him, he'd be stupid not to use her.

But renting the upstairs? Ridiculous. First off, the place was a mess and would take a lot of work to make it livable. Second, he sure didn't need to trade work for rent.

He took out the phone book and looked up Sarah Diamonte's phone number, then dialed. He ground his teeth as he waited, but no one answered. He didn't bother to leave a message.

He'd barely hung up when his cell rang. "This is Jake."

"Hello."

*Rachel.* Her voice was unmistakable. "I just tried to call your mother's to let you know I fixed your tire."

"You fixed it? Oh—my—I mean, thank you so much."

"It's no big deal."

"It is to me. I don't know how to thank you, Jake. I'll pay you back for sure. I just have to—" She stopped, her voice cracking.

"Are you okay?"

Her answer was a long release of air. "Yes. I'm fine. I just don't know when I can come to get it." She cleared her throat. "Oh, before I forget, a couple of people came by with some talk about keeping the bar from opening."

Jake laughed. Ironic. Even those who didn't want him here were convinced he was renovating.

"What's so funny?"

"The idea that a blatant rumor can have half a town believing it's true."

"Maybe there's a reason for that."

"Yeah, like my friends running off at the mouth about it."

"No. More like it's meant to be."

"You mean it's fate?"

"Something like that."

He rolled his head from one side to the other, getting out the kinks in his neck. "I don't believe in fate. We have choices and what we do with those choices determines our future." And he had big choices to make.

"If that's true, I wish I made better decisions."

There was something in her voice that bothered him. She sounded…sad. His pulse kicked up a notch. But…dammit, whatever was wrong, it wasn't his concern. "From what I've seen, how you take care of your daughter, you do quite well."

He heard a long sigh, then the baby gurgling. "Do you want me to drive the van over? I can have a buddy meet me and drive me back."

"No. I couldn't ask you to do that. I'll get a ride over, but it might not be until tomorrow morning."

"Fine."

"I don't know how I can repay you…"

"You can repay me by forgetting about it. *Capisce?*"

At that, he heard a small laugh. "Okay. I'll be there as soon as I can."

"If I'm gone, I'll leave the keys inside."

RACHEL HAD AWAKENED at the crack of dawn, unable to sleep more than an hour at a time on the thin mattress at the Trail's End motel. She hadn't wanted to tell Jake where she was…where her mother had taken her.

At the time, it seemed the only thing to do. She needed a place to stay and it got her mother to leave Jake's place. She didn't want to cause more trouble for Jake. She'd done enough damage fifteen years ago. It was something she'd always carry with her.

"We're going for a ride, sweet pea," she said, dressing Zoe in her pink hooded jacket. Zoe looked so adorable, her blond hair curled around her cherub face. Even though Rachel knew other people saw Zoe as looking different from other babies, to her, Zoe was Zoe.

She glanced at the clock. Barney should be there any second now. The hotel manager had said he'd be happy to drive her to Jake's.

As she finished dressing Zoe, she

heard a horn. Outside, Barney was waiting in his car. "Thank you so much for doing this, Barney."

"No problem," he said. "I know we don't have any rooms available for tonight, but I could probably think of something—if you're interested."

Rachel had the distinct feeling Barney was talking about something more personal. Something not on her radar. Certainly not with him. Room or no room. "I'm good, Barney. I've got someplace to stay, but thanks for the offer." She nearly choked on the words.

Fifteen minutes later when they pulled into the drive at the Wild Card, right next to her VW, Jake was waiting outside. He greeted Barney through his open window and then got down to business.

"The tire is new, I added oil and checked the water and the other tires. I think it's good to go."

"Thank you. I promise I'll pay—"

He held up a hand to stop her. She bit her bottom lip, then got out and walked around to the back for Zoe. Barney came to help, but Jake was there first. He looked at her strangely, probably wondering why Barney had given her a ride.

"Everything okay?" he asked.

She forced a smile. "Everything is fine. In fact, it's great."

He laid one hand on the top of the open door, frowning. "So why don't I believe it?"

She shrugged. "You should believe it, because I'm taking your advice." She lifted Zoe out of her car seat and settled her on one hip.

He reached inside to unlatch the car seat for her. "My advice? I didn't know I'd given any, and if I did, I'm sorry. I'm no one to be giving out advice." He straightened, car seat in hand.

"I'm making a decision and taking charge of my future."

His expression switched from concern to confusion. She didn't know what to make of herself, either. All she knew was that *she* had to be in control. Whatever the end result might be.

"Anything you care to share?"

"No. Right now I need to get my things." She started for the van, waving goodbye to Barney as she did. "Thanks so much."

"No problem," Barney said. "Happy New Year!" Then he backed his car up and slowly turned it around. As he drove away, Jake studied Rachel.

"I thought your plan was to stay at your mother's."

"That changed."

He walked with her, stopped at her vehicle and opened the back door to set the seat inside. "What changed?"

"Do you mind if I go inside and get the things I forgot?"

He stood back, then made a sweeping gesture for her to go ahead.

"And if I could make some calls, I'd appreciate it," she said on the way.

"Calls to find a job or someplace to stay?"

She gave him a long look, then said simply, "Both."

Jake hadn't the foggiest why she and her mother weren't getting along and he didn't care. He wasn't going to get involved. But dammit, he couldn't turn a woman and child into the streets in the middle of winter. On New Year's Eve, no less.

He shoved a hand in his pocket and drew out a handful of twenties. "Here. Take this. Maybe it'll tide you over until you figure out what you're doing."

She hesitated.

"It's only a couple hundred dollars."

He saw her swallow as if she had a rock in her throat. But after a moment, she let out a breath, reached out and took the money.

Rachel Diamonte wouldn't take money from anyone—unless she was desperate. Not the Rachel he'd known in high school. She'd always been proud and stubborn and wanted to be the best.

It had to be a real comedown for her to accept money from someone like him.

"I have to leave to meet some people," he said. "I don't know how easy it's going to be for you to find a place on New Year's Eve, but if you can't, you're welcome to stay here. I probably won't be back until very late anyway."

She opened her mouth but he didn't let her speak. "Uh-uh. Don't say thank-you. I'd do it for anyone. Especially someone with a baby."

He went into his bedroom and found some clean clothes. Brady and Luke had convinced him to bring in the New Year at some bar in San Antonio they said would be filled with single women. They'd hired Miguel, one of Brady's dad's ranch hands, to be their designated driver, so he didn't have to worry about having too much to drink.

Yeah. A night on the town with his buddies was exactly what he needed. A diversion.

After he changed and was on his way

out, he said, "Don't forget to lock up when you leave."

She made an effort to smile, but he wasn't buying it. And he was out of there before he did something stupid. Like offer her a job.

Three hours later, Brady, Luke and Jake had downed three pitchers of margaritas and were working on the fourth. Jake was glad they'd hired Miguel.

Chico's Tex-Mex Cantina in the heart of San Antonio's Riverwalk entertainment complex was "party city" tonight. Sitting at a window, Jake could see the Riverwalk below, crawling with vendors selling the same kinds of tchotchkes they sold in Tijuana. Strolling mariachis played romantic songs to lovers walking hand in hand or smooching in dark corners. In the Cantina, glammed-up singles filed in and out.

"How about her?" Brady asked, lifting his glass in the direction of a redhead baring as much of her attributes as was legal.

"Too tall," Jake answered. "She's more your type." He waggled his eyebrows. "Unless you're saving yourself for the new filly I heard you're seeing. What was her name?"

"The only filly in my life is one I could buy at the upcoming sale," Brady protested. "And, for the record, I'm not saving myself for anyone."

"Hey, hey, hey," Luke cut in. "There's three." He tipped his head toward them. "One for each of us. The brunette for you, Brady buddy, the blonde for Jake the rake since we know he has a thing for certain blondes." He emptied his glass and licked off the salt. "And I'm kinda partial to redheads." He smiled like a satisfied cat. "Whadiyasay?" He started to rise, then seeing no one else did, he dropped back into his chair.

"I say we're pathetic." Jake tipped his chair back on two legs, hands clasped behind his head.

Luke waved the waiter over again. "If Cole weren't head over heels in love with Tessa, and if Blake wasn't being the dutiful dad waiting for Annie to have their kid, we could get things going."

"Like what?" Brady snapped. "Hitting on women that none of us want? There's better pickin's in River Bluff or Bandera at Eleventh Street."

Luke's head came up. "Speak for yourself, dude. There's no one in River Bluff or Bandera I want."

"Except—" Jake wiped the sweat off his glass "—maybe sweet Becky Lynn?"

Luke frowned. "Past tense. Wa-a-ay past tense."

Jake glanced at Brady, who was ogling two women dancing the salsa. "So, Luke where exactly are these three ladies you're talkin' about?"

But he was oblivious to Luke's response. All Jake could think about was a certain blonde with an attitude and a baby, who just might be staying at his place tonight. "I say we call Miguel. I've got better things to do than sit here with you *jamokes*."

Brady and Luke readily agreed and a little more than an hour later, Jake shut the door on the limo and, walking toward the apartment in back, he strained to see if Rachel's van was still there. But it was too dark to tell. He realized then that he was going to be sorely disappointed if she wasn't there.

AWAKENING, RACHEL heard something outside. Footsteps on gravel. Her pulse raced. If it was Jake, she would've heard his car, heard a door slam, wouldn't she? She listened again and the crunching got louder, stopped, then started again.

Quietly, she rolled off the bed so as not to wake Zoe, then glanced around for a weapon of some kind. Finding nothing, she picked up the corner of the curtain and looked out the window. She couldn't see anything in the inky darkness, and the thick pecan grove could hide just about anything. Or anyone.

Maybe it was just an animal and she was imagining she'd heard footsteps.

Still searching for something to use in self-defense, the only thing she could find was one of Jake's shoes. Quickly she snatched it up and stood, back to the wall, beside the door.

The handle turned, then she heard a click and the door slowly inched open. Her heart pounded. The nightlight gave off a low glow, but it was enough for her to see. Dark hair. *Jake*. She sagged in relief.

He smiled, and just as he opened his mouth to speak, she put her index finger to her lips. "Shh. I don't want to wake Zoe. But you scared me half to death. I didn't hear a car."

"Sorry," Jake said, keeping his voice low.

There was liquor on his breath. "You're drunk."

"Not drunk," he whispered, "just—happy." He gave her a silly-ass grin.

She couldn't help but smile. "It's good that you were smart enough to get a ride."

"So," he whispered, "I guess you didn't find a place to stay."

"Uh, yeah. Everything in River Bluff is booked for tonight."

Just then he reached up and touched her cheek. "You know, you really haven't changed that much in all these years."

Rachel knew better.

"You may not think you're drunk," she said. "But something has affected your eyesight."

His gaze traveled from her hair to her eyes to her mouth and back again. "No, it's true." He took her hand and pulled her across the living room and into the doorway to the bar.

"Tell me," he said, gesturing inside, "what do you really think? Can this place be restored without breaking the bank?" He flipped the light switch.

The one yellowed bulb in the chandelier cast a sepia glow. Rachel scanned the room before walking across to the other side, navigating the debris on the way. She picked up a piece of paper, rubbed some of the dust on the bar with it, then ran her fingers over the carved design.

"It's mahogany," Jake said. "It was beautiful at one time."

"It could be again." She looked up at the chandelier. "That's a great piece, too. It needs work, but I think it would be worth it. Preserving as much of the original construction as possible will help maintain its authenticity." She walked back to where he stood, leaning casually against the archway, his weight on one foot.

His dark hair looped over his forehead; and his eyelids, half-closed, gave him a sleepy, dreamy look, making her blood race through her veins. Standing close, she raised her chin. "But I'm sure you know, renovation is only the beginning."

He reached out and touched her nose. "Dust," he said. His fingers lingered there, then he traced a path down her jawline to her neck. And, as if it was the most natural thing in the world, he slipped his hand under her hair at the back of her neck and gently drew her to him. His mouth closed over hers.

He'd barely brushed her lips in a featherlight kiss before she closed her eyes and melted against him. She should stop. He was drunk, his inhibitions down. He didn't know what he was doing. But even though she hadn't had a drop to drink, her inhibitions seemed equally nonexistent. She felt a pull deep in her belly. A gnawing, physical hunger.

She realized at precisely the moment he pulled away, how much she wanted him.

He stepped back and, with a goofy look on his face, he shoved a hand through his hair. "I—I don't know why I did that."

That wasn't what she'd wanted him to say. "I do," she said, noticing the confetti on his shirt, a smudge of lipstick on his cheek—the reminders of a New Year's

Eve party? "You've had too much to drink." But *she* had no excuse, other than being desperate for the touch of another human being…someone other than her baby. "Let's call it a New Year's kiss and forget about it." She slipped around him and went back into the apartment.

"I'll—um—I'll sleep on the couch," Jake tossed out.

"Okay," she said without looking back, tears filling her eyes. She hurried into the bedroom and quietly crawled in beside Zoe. Lord, she didn't know what was wrong with her.

With her head on Jake's pillow, breathing in his scent, she bit her bottom lip, hoping to hold the tears at bay. And when she couldn't, she covered her mouth like she used to as a child, to make sure she didn't make any noise when she cried.

# *CHAPTER EIGHT*

LIGHT FILTERED THROUGH the flimsy white curtains. It had to be close to eight, Jake realized and sat upright on the couch. He shook his head, vaguely remembering the night before. Rachel. She'd been here. He glanced toward the kitchen. Everything was dead quiet.

His head throbbed when he stood, and he remembered all the margaritas they'd consumed in San Antonio. And, if he remembered correctly, his truck was still at Brady's.

On his way to the john, he stopped at the bedroom and, hearing nothing, he peeked inside. The bed was made and there was no sign that anyone had been there. He spun around, scanning the kitchen. The little pink blanket that had been on the table was gone, along with Rachel's portfolio.

For a second, he hoped he was wrong, that she was outside or something. Then just as quickly he realized how stupid that was.

Somewhere in his foggy brain, he remembered soft warm lips and Rachel's feminine body molded against his. And he was pretty sure *that* hadn't been a dream.

He went to the window. The VW was gone. Dammit. He'd wanted to tell her about the tire and…something else. Or maybe he just wanted her to be here. He'd actually enjoyed making breakfast for her the day before.

He headed for the bathroom and when he finished, he took a quick shower. He'd have to ride his Harley to the charity benefit since his truck was still at Brady's. He'd figure out how to get it later. If it was just another party, he'd blow it off. But a benefit for kids was different. He'd stay just long enough to satisfy his buddies, and then he'd leave.

He wished Cole, his best friend all through school, was back from Oregon. He needed to talk. He needed a sounding board, and Cole was the one who most understood where he was coming from.

They'd been tight through school, both without fathers, Cole because his dad had killed himself and Jake because his father had run off or didn't want to acknowledge paternity. Either way, the result was the same. He and Cole had been two angry kids against the world.

All these years, he'd wanted to see the Wild Bunch, but couldn't bring himself to go back to River Bluff. And then when he'd finally returned for Blake's wedding and Uncle Verne's funeral, Cole had seemed distant. Supportive, like all the guys, but distant. As if he had something on his mind about Jake. Something he wasn't ready to say.

Jake hoped Cole got back before he

left for California. There was a lot they both needed to get off their chests.

He stuffed his legs into his jeans, threw on a black cotton sweater, his boots and leather jacket and went into the bar and turned on the lights. His gaze drifted to his mom's Paris poster.

That's when he realized why he'd been reluctant to leave. The Wild Card had been his mother's dream. Once, he'd heard his mother tell Woody that the Wild Card was the only thing she had to leave her son. She wanted the Wild Card to be a success—not just so she could go to Paris, but for Jake. He pulled in a deep breath and glanced around. Rachel thought the place was worth renovating, but that was a designer's perspective. As a businessman, he knew better than to make decisions based on emotions. It had to make good financial sense.

The sun was out and, as he walked around the property, he felt good. He went back inside, got out his laptop and pulled up his accounts for Tellmell.com.

The company was going strong, but ever since his first partner sold information to a rival company, Jake personally monitored the security system. He'd never totally entrust his business to someone else again. But, still, the company practically ran itself now.

Jake almost longed for the days when he was scrambling to make his business a success. Back then, he'd been infused with energy and excitement, and the possibilities had felt endless. The idea of reopening the Card had started to make him feel that way again.

He tended to business for the next few hours and made "Happy New Year" phone calls to his top management and their families, but through it all, he kept wondering if Rachel and her baby were okay. Where had she gone? To a motel? To her mother's? Maybe she'd called a friend?

It occurred to him that Rachel might be at the charity benefit, too—which, he realized had already started.

He shut off his laptop, changed into a dress shirt and jacket, grabbed his helmet and was out the door.

On the road, his mind hummed as fast as the motor on his Harley.

"YOU SHOULD GO," Becky said to Rachel. "Everyone goes to the charity benefit."

"Everyone who's invited."

"But they would've invited you if they knew you were here."

"Everyone knows I'm here. My mother said so." Rachel picked up her cup and took a sip of tea. When she'd run into Becky after leaving Jake's, Becky had invited her to breakfast at her house. Rachel was grateful for the invitation, and hoped that later she'd be able to get a room at the motel again.

But for now, Zoe was happily playing on a blanket on the floor and Rachel couldn't help thinking how nice it would be to have a place of her own. The blinking lights on Becky's Christmas tree kept Zoe occupied. Zoe hadn't started crawling yet, her motor development slow as it was with many Down children, but her vision hadn't been affected like some and Rachel was grateful for that.

Becky pursed her lips. "An oversight. Besides, no one would know how to get in touch with you, would they?" She grinned. "You could go anyway, though. It's a standing invitation to anyone in town."

"I'd rather not," Rachel said. "Zoe hasn't been around a lot of people in a party atmosphere like that and she could get scared."

"What about a sitter, then? If I wasn't working today, I'd love to watch her for you."

"Becky," Rachel said firmly, "quit worrying about it. I'm fine with not going. I'd hate to run into my mother, and I have a ton of things to do. I just wish it wasn't a holiday today, so I could do them."

Becky leaned forward, elbows on the table. "There are—people I don't want to run into, either. So, getting back to you, your mother never told anyone that you two weren't getting along."

Rachel handed Zoe a toy. "That's my mother. Always worried about appearances." She sighed. "I probably shouldn't have said anything."

Becky narrowed her eyes. "I'm going to be honest here. Okay?"

Rachel nodded.

"Not saying anything is why you got the reputation of being stuck-up in school. You never talked to anyone about anything." She cleared her throat. "Well, except for that one time you told me about Luke," she said almost under her breath. "You gave everyone the impression you thought you were better than them."

Rachel's mouth dropped open. "Wow. And I thought everyone liked me. I didn't have a lot of close friends because I didn't have time to do things outside of school activities, but I didn't know everyone thought I was stuck-up."

Wrinkling her nose as if hesitant to continue, Becky said, "You didn't know because you never talked to anyone. You never got close enough to find out." She cleared her throat. "Jake used to have this ditty he sang about you. I can't remember it now, but it was funny."

Rachel felt the air leave her lungs. She'd been a cheerleader, the class president, the homecoming queen. How could her classmates not like her? And Jake had made fun of her when she'd been mooning over him.

"Damn. That truly sucks," she said and, half-joking, threw up her hands and sagged against the back of the chair. "Well, Kyle liked me."

"Yeah, and that turned out well, didn't it?"

Rachel had asked for that. Kyle had screwed her over and left town. And according to Becky, no one had heard from him since.

"But that was then," Becky added. "You're different now."

Was she? Really? "Well, speaking of now, I've got to get busy and find a job." The money Jake had given her would last a couple of nights at the Trail's End if she could get another room…or she could use most of it to promote herself as an interior designer and hope she'd get a job out of it.

"What are you planning?"

"I brought my laptop with me, so I'm going to design some flyers offering my services, find somewhere to print them out and distribute them. I'm not sure how to do that, but I'll think of something."

"I have a printer," Becky said, her eyes lighting up. "You design it right now, then ask at the newspaper tomorrow if you can put one in each issue. I know some of the other businesses do that."

"That's a great idea. But won't they charge for that?"

Becky shrugged. "Annie—you remember Cole's sister—she writes for the

*River's Run* and I know she does a lot of stories on people in town publicizing different things. Maybe she can write one on the kind of work you do—"

"I can't wait for maybes, Becky. The flyer seems the fastest, least expensive way to go." She'd hand them out door to door if she had to. "Maybe if I put a coupon on the flyer for a discount, that'll give people an incentive."

"And you might want to get the flyer in the *San Antonio Express-News*, too."

"Anywhere I can. If I could get someone, a teenager maybe, to distribute flyers to all the homes and businesses in River Bluff, Bandera and even San Antonio, it might not cost too much."

"I'd volunteer Shane, but he doesn't have the time. Maybe he could ask around if any of his friends need some work."

"Thanks. I'll start with the newspaper first." If she could get her name out there, if she got even one job, it would be a start. But what would she do until then? Nothing was likely to happen before the money Jake gave her ran out.

"So, let's get busy," Becky said. "I've got to leave in a few, but I could drop one off at Annie's and ask her advice."

"I thought she married someone in San Antonio."

Becky nodded. "She did. Blake Smith. Then he disappeared and she got an annulment. It's a long story. Bottom line is they ended up together again and they're going to have a baby. Blake plays poker with the Wild Bunch."

Rachel smiled wistfully. She wished she had a group of friends as tight as the Wild Bunch. But now it turns out she had no one—and never had. At least not since her father died. Oddly, that news didn't bother her nearly as much as the revelation that Jake used to make fun of her.

"Okay, then," she forced out. "I'll get my laptop."

JAKE HEARD THE MUSIC long before he reached the River Bluff High School auditorium. Outside, there had to be close to the two hundred cars Ed had told him they'd prepared for. Toward the back, a large canvas canopy covered a makeshift bar. Alcohol wasn't allowed inside the school, good cause notwithstanding.

Walking inside, the twang of country music assaulted him. The last charity shindig he'd been to had been a formal affair in San Diego at the Westgate Hotel, with a full-string orchestra playing Rachmaninoff.

Here, the instruments were guitars and the Lonely Coyote Band was playing its rendition of "Friends in Low Places." Instead of tuxedos, the men wore their best Western dinner jackets, bolo ties and cowboy boots. The women's attire was all over the place from flowing pants to slinky gowns. Jake wore the same black sport jacket, white dress shirt, black jeans and boots that he'd worn for his uncle's funeral. What mattered was the money he'd donated and that he showed up. Showing up meant a lot in River Bluff.

Picking his way through the crowd to reach the bar outside, he searched for his friends. Just as he saw Blake across the room talking to Brady, he felt someone nudge him.

"Can you believe this?" Luke said. "I bet Mike is as happy as a pig in—"

"I'm not stayin' long," Jake said. "I'm only here to get my truck…and because you guys blackmailed me."

"Hoo, yeah! That blackmail did work, didn't it," Luke said. "I'll have to remember that the next time I want you to do something. Just threaten to tell Rachel how you carved her initials in the—"

"You want to play dirty? I got a hundred says you can't get a date with Becky Lynn."

Luke's expression went dark.

Jake pulled back, looking at his buddy

in surprise. "Hey, I'm sorry. Don't tell me you've still got a thing for Becky?"

"Hell, no. I haven't even talked to her since I've been back from Iraq."

"I just saw Hank come in," Jake said, changing the topic, troubled that he may have hurt his friend.

"C'mon." Luke elbowed him. "I need a drink."

On their way back from the bar, Jake and Luke took a sharp turn to the right to talk to Brady and Blake who stood near the stage where the band was tuning up. The two were laughing their fool heads off.

"Okay, what's going on?" Jake asked. "You guys getting a poker game going in the lunchroom?"

While they sparred and joked, Jake kept scanning the crowd to see who showed up next. One person he was hoping not to run into, and another, he realized, he was hoping might show up.

"I think Jake's the one who's got

something on his mind," Luke said. "Like finding a certain woman?"

"Yep. Any woman," he replied, not missing a beat. "If she's pretty and has a brain, I'm ready." He didn't expect Luke to believe that crap any more than he did, but what else could he say?

"Yeah, I'm ready, too," Luke chimed in over the music. The two headed toward the back door, sidestepping couples, young and old, on the dance floor.

Outside, the bartender, who wore a ponytail and Navajo red boots, looked as if he'd just come off a Western movie set. "I'll have the coldest soda you got," Jake said.

"Hey, there's Hank again," Jake said to Luke. "You two getting along any better?"

Luke turned the other way so he was facing away from Hank. "Nothing's changed. He's still an ass."

"Why don't you just talk it out?"

"There's nothin' to talk about. He was

sixteen when I was adopted, and he's had an attitude ever since."

They discussed Luke's dad's health and then suddenly Luke waved at someone. Jake followed Luke's line of sight and saw Annie talking to Sarah Diamonte. Rachel's mother was older, but she had the same unsmiling face, the same unkind eyes. Jake would've gone over to congratulate Annie on her pregnancy, but not with Sarah at her side.

Jake saw Brady walk over and kiss Annie, and then they all looked at the paper she was holding. Mrs. Diamonte grabbed the paper, then folded it in half. When Annie and Brady left, she crumpled the paper in a ball and tossed it into the basket beside her.

"I'm getting hungry," Luke said. "Let's check out the food." He started off in the opposite direction.

"Not a bad idea." But Jake hadn't taken more than two steps when he heard Brady behind him. "Jake, wait up."

Jake turned.

"Look at this," Brady said, handing him a flyer.

Jake quickly scanned the paper. Hiding his surprise, he handed it back. "Thanks, but no thanks."

Brady shrugged, and Jake went to catch up with Luke at one of the long buffet tables. So Rachel was setting up business here in River Bluff. Good for her. But was he ready to be one of her first clients? Was his mother's memory good enough reason for him to sink money into a town he wanted nothing to do with? If the Wild Card was a tourist draw, he'd be contributing to the economy of a place he hated.

Jake found a plate and as he was heaping it with barbecued pork, coleslaw, Texas beans and homemade biscuits, he heard someone behind him mention the Wild Card.

He turned and, off to the side behind a post, saw Brady's father, Marshall Carrick, talking to Wade Barstow. Barstow's back was to Jake. Even if he hadn't seen him at the café, he would've known him at a glance. Fifteen years might've added some silver to his hair, but time hadn't changed the tall man's broad shoulders or commanding presence. While Jake watched, a younger woman came over to Barstow, gave him a kiss and stood there with the two men.

With the post between them, Jake knew they hadn't seen him, and Marshall Carrick just kept on talking. As Jake moved down the food line, he heard him say, "Those were the days. But it would take a lot to get the Wild Card up and running again."

"I have fond memories of that place," Barstow said.

Carrick nudged him. "I bet you do."

They both laughed heartily. "So," Carrick said, "when do you think you'll seal the deal for the property?"

"The sooner the better," Barstow responded. "I've got a lot riding on that property. My guy Dempsey is a good negotiator. He'll make Lola's boy an offer he can't refuse. It'll get done, one way or another."

"You should consider renovating. We need a place like that again."

Barstow nodded. "I'm not sure what I'm going to do with it, but that's definitely one consideration."

Jake's nerves drew tight. *Lola's boy*. His blood felt like steam in his veins. Barstow talked as if it was a fait accompli. And if Jake didn't get out of here, he was pretty certain he'd say or do something he'd regret.

He sat with Luke who'd seen Marshall with Barstow, but had been too far away to hear. "Who's the woman?" Jake asked.

"His wife. Kitty divorced him and, not long after Kyle left, she moved away and Wade remarried."

Jake clenched his jaws. Apparently Lola Chandler was good enough for Barstow to sleep with, but not good enough to marry.

He tried to eat, but what should have

been delicious tasted like sawdust in his mouth. Finally, he pushed his food away, told Luke he had to leave. He found Luke's folks, who were now standing near Brady's dad and mother, Marshall and Angela Carrick. "Thanks for the invite on Christmas Day," Jake said to the Chisums. "It's great to see everyone again."

"Great to see you, too," Lucy Chisum said.

Marshall leaned in and said, "I guess I'll see you on Wednesday. Brady said it's his turn to host poker night."

"I don't know why you're wasting your time this way," Angela piped up, slurring slightly.

Jake had heard rumors that Angela Carrick had a drinking problem. He wasn't one to believe rumors, but maybe this one had some basis in fact.

"Do you have to play at *that* place again?" she muttered.

*That place*. Meaning the Wild Card. Jake shoved his hands into his pockets.

But Angela Carrick was Brady's mother and Jake wasn't about to be disrespectful.

He did wonder how she'd feel if he told her he might be renovating the place. Wondered how they'd all feel. Jake knew from listening to the men when he was a child that Marshall Carrick had never had any qualms about staying at the Wild Card until the early hours.

Someone came up behind Marshall and he nodded his goodbye to Jake before turning away.

"Well, thanks again, Mrs. Carrick," Jake said as cheerfully as he could manage. "Please tell Brady I'll see him on Wednesday."

The fire in her eyes told him he'd overstayed his welcome, so he gave her a two-finger salute and then he was outta there.

Jake fumed all the way home. He was sick of feigned politeness, fake smiles and insincere handshakes. And he hated that it bothered him enough to get angry about it. He hated that he had any feelings at all about the people of River Bluff. He shouldn't give a rat's ass about who bought the Wild Card, who renovated it, or tore it to the ground for that matter.

What did matter was his business and his life in California. He had everything he wanted there. It wasn't perfect, but then what was?

Back home, he went inside, took out a beer, headed into the bar, pulled down a dusty chair and plunked it in the middle of the room.

He'd actually believed selling the Card would give him closure. Now, he knew better—because he'd finally realized that what he hated wasn't the town. It was how his mother had been judged, how she'd been treated as if she were a cancer to be cut out. In the end, the cancer had gotten her.

He'd wanted closure, but how did a person ever find closure on that?

Selling the Wild Card wasn't going to

change anything. He didn't know what would.

The phone rang and when he looked at the call display, he saw it was Barstow's attorney. Great. Just great.

Leaning back in the chair, he answered, "This is Jake."

"Dempsey here. I thought I'd check with you on our meeting time for tomorrow."

Jake took a swig of beer. "Yeah, about that meeting."

# CHAPTER NINE

SITTING ON THE SAGGING, wafer-thin mattress, Rachel glanced around the cheap motel room. At least it was a roof over their heads...for a couple of days.

After doing exercises with Zoe, then playing "Itsy Bitsy Spider," Rachel decided to get some fresh air and exercise for herself. Everyone in Bandera County would be at the charity benefit, so wherever she went, she'd most likely have the place to herself.

She buckled Zoe into the van and started driving. The countryside was so beautiful, almost anywhere she could find a sidewalk for Zoe's stroller would be fine.

Seeing a turnoff, she headed toward

the Medina River, and another of the places the kids used to go to make out in high school.

Finding a spot, she parked, got out Zoe's stroller, tucked her in, then followed the path to the river. The trees were denser than she remembered, the walkway not as big. And since it was winter the grass was brown in spots and there were no flowers.

"This will be fun, Zoe. Smell that air." Scented with burning cedar from someone's fireplace, the air was fresh, not hot and humid like the one and only time she'd been here—the night Trevor Paxton had left her crying, her blouse ripped down the front and hanging off her shoulder. Jake had been swimming in another spot and hearing the commotion, he'd come up behind her, scaring her half to death.

"Are you hurt?" he'd asked.

She'd swirled around, holding the tattered remnants of her shirt against her chest, then seeing who it was, she shook her head. Immediately he handed her the

T-shirt he held in his hand, then he looked down the road at the car speeding away. "Who was that?"

She shook her head again. She couldn't say. It would be worse for her if she did and her parents found out. But she couldn't stop shaking. When he'd reached up and brushed a tear from her cheek, she'd wanted to bawl.

"I'll take you home," he'd said without hesitation. "My bike is over there where I was swimming."

She could tell he'd been in the water because his long brandy-colored hair was wet and unruly, as if he'd combed it with his fingers. The moonlight had played off his smooth, olive skin. She'd seen the moon reflected in his eyes, making the brown color almost gold, and when he'd looked at her, she'd felt as if he could see into her soul.

Riding behind him, she'd felt the hot Texas air slide across her face like a long silk scarf, the wind in her hair seductive with the scent of magnolias. With her arms wrapped around Jake's chest, her face pressed against his skin, still moist from the river, her body against his, she'd wanted to keep on riding forever.

Jake had waited until she got in the door when they'd reached her house, but before he could leave, her mother had come out and wailed on him. "I'll press charges!" she'd shouted. "You can't do this to my daughter."

Jake had gone without saying a word in protest.

She'd worn his T-shirt to bed that night and kept it for months until her mother found it. Her mother never believed Jake was innocent, mainly because Rachel couldn't bring herself to tell her parents that she'd been at the river with Trevor.

She'd wanted to rebel, wanted to be like the other girls and she'd led the boy to believe that she wanted him to be the first. When she'd had second thoughts, he'd tried to force her. If Jake hadn't come along, it might've been worse.

She hadn't found out until years later that Trevor had called her mother and ratted Jake out—falsely, of course.

And that wasn't even the night that made Jake hate her so much. It was the night of the fire that changed everything, and she'd give anything if she could relive that night and do things differently. But she couldn't. All the years of hurt couldn't be undone.

Then, as if she'd asked the past to come alive, she saw a man coming up the narrow path from the river. She caught her breath. Her heart thudded.

But it wasn't Jake. It was a teenager she didn't know.

She said hello, but he only nodded shyly and went on his way.

She sat on the bench with Zoe, but her mind wandered. She'd felt a letdown when she'd left the Wild Card this morning, and the feeling had persisted all day.

She didn't feel positive and determined anymore. She didn't know what was going to happen. If her flyers didn't work… She and Zoe might end up homeless on the street. And she'd be the failure her mother always said she was.

THE NEXT MORNING, as Jake rounded the corner on Main on his Harley, he saw Cole's truck parked across the street from Harry's Hardware store. It buoyed his spirits. He hadn't heard Cole was back. He parked in front of the store and went inside, his adrenaline pumping. He was about to do the stupidest thing of his life.

Cole stood at the counter in the hardware section of the store, his back to Jake, talking with Sally Knutson, Harry's wife. Sally ran the only beauty shop in town and it was connected to the hardware store the couple owned. You could access the beauty shop from inside the hardware store or outside on the street.

Jake smiled seeing a poster above the door leading into the beauty shop that depicted a scene from the movie *When Harry Met Sally* and the caption, "I'll have what she's having." Sally had superimposed a funky hairdo on Meg Ryan and the words, "Get the haircut *you* want! $19.99—Shampoo, Cut and Style."

At least someone in this town had a sense of humor. "Jake, how are you honey?" Sally said in her deep smoker's voice.

Cole turned.

"Mornin', Sally. Sorry I missed you at the party yesterday." Jake nodded to Cole, then broke into a big smile. "Hey, buddy. Glad you're back." He reached to shake hands and nudged Cole on the shoulder at the same time. "Tessa come with you?"

"She's still in Oregon settling her business affairs. I'm heading there again in a couple of days, then we'll drive a U-Haul back to River Bluff. What's up?"

"I need to talk when you have some time."

Cole brought himself up, squared his shoulders. "Sure. What about?"

Jake looked at Sally, who was all ears. She picked up one of the three cats circling her legs. "Hello, adorable. You're just the sweetest little thing, aren't you?"

Motioning Cole toward the door, Jake stepped back. "I need some advice."

Cole turned to Sally. "Tell Harry I'll check back later on that order."

"Bye, Sally," Jake said, waving as he followed Cole out. He got the distinct impression his friend was out of sorts. He hoped it wasn't something with Tessa and their plans to get married.

Once outside, Cole strode to the grassy area behind his truck, a little city park with a bandstand in the center. Jake remembered singing Christmas carols there one year with his class.

Cole stood feet apart, arms crossed over his chest. "I'm not the best person to give advice, you know."

"In this case, I think you are."

Cole stared at Jake, his body rigid.

"You're the expert on construction," Jake began. "What would I need to do to get started on the Wild Card?" Jake shoved his hands into his pockets, his nerves humming now that he'd finally put voice to his thoughts. Thoughts that might tie him to a place he didn't want to be. "*If* I were going to do it."

Cole's lips thinned. "My advice," he said succinctly, "is make up your damned mind."

What the hell… Jake held out his hands, palms up. "Something I'm missing here?"

Cole rubbed the back of his neck. "Yeah. I'm *not* going to get excited about an idea that might never happen, that's what you're missing."

Jake's muscles felt like knots under his skin.

Cole swung around, antsy, pacing. Then he stopped in front of Jake again, face-to-face. "I got excited before. All our plans, all that talk about sticking together—starting a business—and then you took off." Cole pointed in Jake's face. "You freaking took off."

Adrenaline shot through Jake's veins. "Yeah, but you have to understand—"

"That's the thing. There wasn't anything *to* understand! It pissed me off. Not a word, Jake! Nothing. Fifteen years. Hell, I thought something happened. I thought you were dead." He banged his hand on the tailgate.

*Dead. Like your dad.* Jake felt as if he'd been punched in the gut.

"Do you know what that feels like?"

"Oh, man." Jake looked down, anywhere but at Cole. "I'm an idiot." He couldn't have felt lower if he were a snake. He shoved a hand through his hair. "But I couldn't stay. Not after the fire." He couldn't stand that he'd hurt Cole.

"I should've told you," Jake continued. "Dammit. I should have and I didn't. I didn't because the only person I was thinking about was me." And saying he was sorry wouldn't make up for it. Jake knew Cole. He let things fester. Fifteen years was a long time to let something fester.

Cole glared, a muscle twitched at his temple.

"Why don't you just punch me and get it over with," Jake said.

"Don't be stupid."

"Go ahead. Punch me," Jake said, sticking out his chin, egging him on. "Or are you all talk and no action." He shoved Cole just enough to make it real.

Fire shone in Cole's eyes. He slapped a hand against Jake's chest and shoved back. Jake lunged forward and within a heartbeat Cole had sidestepped him, then jabbed, landing a soft punch. Jake jabbed back. Cole lunged again. Jake grabbed him in a bear hug. They swung around, banging against the truck and then hitting the ground, with Cole ending up on Jake's chest, his fist drawn for a punch that might actually connect. Before he got it off, he stopped. They both burst out laughing. "Shit," Cole said and rolled onto the grass and dirt next to Jake, both still laughing.

Finally, Cole stood and, breathing heavily, he extended his hand to Jake. Jake spit grass and dirt from his mouth as he got up. Cole dusted himself off, and when the two looked up, a crowd had gathered around them, including Sally and Harold Knutson.

"Disgusting," one woman said.

"Still the same," someone whispered behind Jake. "Won't they ever grow up?"

"What are you all looking at?" Cole snapped. "A guy can't have any fun around here anymore?"

Sally shook her head. "You boys are something else."

The crowd dispersed and Jake and Cole stood there facing each other. "You still fight like a girl," Cole said.

"Takes one to know one," Jake countered.

"So, when do we start the renovation?"

RISING EARLY, Rachel took out the cereal and the milk she kept in her cooler and poured a bowl for herself. "Here, sweetie," she said, placing a few Cheerios on the portable tray she'd attached to Zoe's chair. Rachel took every opportunity to help Zoe improve her fine-motor movements, one of the developmental problems in children with Down syndrome. Zoe pushed at the Cheerios rather than grabbing them. When she moved her fingers as if she might actually pick one up, Rachel's pulse raced. Giving her food to handle was more of an exercise than anything, but every little step forward felt like a major achievement. "I'll have your breakfast ready in just a few minutes," she said, as if Zoe understood.

When they finished eating, Rachel checked her money—enough for one more night at the motel, and a little left over to circulate the flyers with the newspaper. If it didn't cost too much.

She picked up the disposable cell Jake

had left in her vehicle, reminded again of his kindness when he shouldn't be kind, and then stuffed it into her purse. For the life of her, she couldn't figure out why he bothered. She'd ruined his life for God's sake. At least the one he'd planned on having, or so he'd said that night in the grove before he'd left town.

Ten minutes later, Rachel walked into the River Bluff newspaper office. The place, an open room inside except for a half wall that separated the entry from a couple of desks in the back, looked deserted. "Hello," she called out, then set Zoe's seat on the floor. "Anyone here?"

"Just a minute!" A woman's voice called from another room.

Rachel quickly fluffed her hair, hoping she didn't look too unprofessional. She'd used the motel's iron to press out the folds in her navy business suit and the white knit shirt she'd gotten out of one of the boxes in the back of her van. She'd pulled her hair back with a hair clip and put on her small, gold hoop earrings—the best she could do under the circumstances.

When the woman behind the voice appeared, she recognized Annie Lawry immediately. Annie Smith now, according to Becky. And she looked wonderful.

"Rachel," Annie said, her eyes lighting up. "Becky told me you were back. How are you?" She reached out a hand.

Rachel smiled at the welcome, which seemed a lot friendlier than any she'd ever gotten from Annie in high school. "I'm fine, Annie. How are you?"

"Good. Very good." The woman practically glowed. She motioned to a desk in the corner. "Come on in. I've already asked about the flyers and Fred agreed to distribute them with the paper. But we only have extra people hired to do those things one day a week. Usually on Mondays."

*Six days from now*. Rachel hadn't

thought of that. She'd hoped to get the flyers out immediately. She picked up Zoe and followed Annie to her desk.

"Oh, you have your baby along." She leaned down, smiling at Zoe. "Hello, darling."

Zoe gurgled and kicked her feet.

"Becky told me you had a daughter. She's so cute."

Before Rachel could answer, Annie said, "Sit down. We need to catch up. It's been a long time."

It was. But as much as Rachel wanted to sit and chat, all she could think about was how she was going to get her flyers out before next Monday and how she was going to pay for it. She took Zoe from her seat and held her in her lap. "Do you know how much it will cost?"

"No, but I can find our price list. We don't do much except want ads and some local business promotions." She rummaged through a drawer. "Ah, here it is." She handed Rachel a sheet of paper. "I don't think Fred has ever used that list."

Rachel glanced at the figures. It wasn't much, and she had the money…if she didn't get a room. Her stomach knotted.

A bell rang and the front door opened. It was Jake.

"Hi, Jake," Annie said.

"Hi, Annie," Jake said looking at Rachel, then back to Annie. "How are you?"

"I'm wonderful." Smiling, Annie pressed a hand to her belly. "What can I do for you?"

"Nothing, Annie." He turned to Rachel, then said softly, "I saw your car outside, Rachel, and I'd like to talk to you for a minute."

Rachel stood, Zoe still in her arms. "Sure. What is it?"

"Outside?"

"Look," Annie piped up, "if you want privacy, use Mike's office. He's not here."

Rachel was about to follow Jake when Annie said, "Here, let me take her. I need the practice."

"Are you—" Rachel said, but didn't finish because she saw the beaming expression on Annie's face.

"I am. And I can't wait," Annie said. "Just leave your little angel with me and I'll be happy."

Zoe gurgled and squealed as she took her from Rachel's arms.

Jake held the door as Rachel went into the next room and then shut it behind them. The room was small, with no windows. Claustrophobic.

"What's up?" Rachel asked.

He had the strangest look in his eyes. He crossed his arms and sat on the edge of the publisher's old oak desk, feet out. "I'm going to do it."

She waited for the rest. Did he mean what she thought he did, and if so, why was he telling her? Unless… Suddenly she couldn't breathe. "Wh-what are you going to do?"

"The Wild Card." He stood again, started pacing. "I'm going to renovate the Wild Card."

He stopped in front of her, then smiled.

Did she dare hope he had a reason for telling her? "And?" She moistened her lips.

"*And* I need your help."

It took a moment for it to sink in. "My help—as in design help?"

"From conception to finish. I need great work if I'm going to pull this off."

Now she really couldn't breathe. "Starting when?"

"Whenever you can. I need to get a building permit. But first I need estimates. This is going to be Cole's first job in his new business. He's coming out to the Wild Card this afternoon. If you can come, too, we can start planning."

When she didn't say anything, he said, "Are you on board?" He sat on the edge of the desk again. "I know we need to talk money, so think about that, too. I want a good product and I'm willing to pay for it."

She chewed on her bottom lip. "Can I use the upstairs apartment?"

He crossed his arms, frowning. "You drive a hard bargain."

She shrugged. "Starting today?"

Abruptly he stood and walked to the door.

Her heart sank.

One hand on the knob, he turned and said, "How about tomorrow? I'm having a poker game tonight and it'll probably get loud."

She had money for the motel, she couldn't say no. "Okay. Then when do you want to start working?"

"Can you be there in an hour?"

She sucked in a gulp of air. She could be there in ten minutes if she had to. Glancing at her watch, she said, "Yes, I believe I can."

He reached into his jacket pocket and pulled out a key. "Here's a key. I have to make a couple of stops. If you get there before I do, just make yourself comfortable."

As she took the key, her heart felt as if it might leap from her chest. She started to say thanks, but he was gone.

She leaned against the desk, her heart drumming in her ears. She had a job. She had a place to live. Thank God. She wanted to jump up and down.

Grinning from ear to ear, she rushed back into the room, took Zoe from Annie and swung her around. "Zoe, Zoe, Zoe. Things are going to be great!"

Annie smiled. "I take it something good happened?"

"Something wonderful," Rachel said. "I have my first gig in River Bluff."

"Is this a story?" Annie asked. "Is Jake going to renovate the Wild Card? I've heard the rumor, but Blake keeps saying—"

Rachel shook her head. "Forget I said anything." If she knew nothing else, she knew Jake hated the way rumors spread in River Bluff, and she didn't want to make him angry before she even started work. If he wanted to tell people, that was up to him.

"Well, *I* think we have a story," Annie said. "I just need verification."

# CHAPTER TEN

JAKE WENT DIRECTLY to the River Bluff Wells Fargo Bank, a small branch of the parent company in San Antonio. He could just as easily open an account while he was in San Antonio getting his building permit tomorrow, but working with locals was always a good business practice.

Just as he shouldered open the door, someone started coming out. Raising his gaze, he stood eyeball-to-eyeball with Wade Barstow.

Neither man stepped aside. Barstow nodded. "Mornin', Jake."

Jake lifted his chin in acknowledgment. It was all he could manage.

"I spoke with my attorney," Barstow

said. "I'm sorry we couldn't come to an agreement. I'm still open to making a deal. Just let me know your price."

Jake felt like punching the guy. "There is no price. I believe I was clear with Mr. Dempsey."

Barstow set his teeth. "The place is an eyesore. The property could be put to better use."

Jake smiled. "Well, then we're both on the same page. I'm starting renovations this week."

The man's expression didn't change.

A good poker face, Jake decided, then remembered how he'd watched Barstow and his cronies playing Hold'em at the saloon way back when. Back when Jake's mother was alive.

Just then a woman came up behind Barstow. The redhead from the party. His wife.

"Okay, Wade. I'm done here," she said, before realizing her husband wasn't alone. "Oh, I'm sorry. I didn't mean to interrupt." She reached out a hand. "Hi, I'm Ellie, Wade's wife."

Jake cleared his throat and shook her hand. "Pleased to meet you, ma'am."

"This is Jake Chandler," Barstow said, as if she'd already heard of him.

Ellie's smile broadened. "Oh, yes. You own the old saloon. Wade has told me all about the old days and how much fun he had when it was open." She looked up at her husband, then to Jake. "I'm so glad he's finally getting his wish to buy the property. I can't wait until—"

Barstow took her by the arm and urged her out the door.

Jake waited for a second, fighting back his anger. He turned to go about his business, only to see both bank employees gaping at him.

"All right," he said, and rubbed his hands together. "Who wants to help me open an account?"

RACHEL PULLED INTO the drive at the saloon and saw Cole Lawry sitting on the porch steps, his back against the weathered rail, Cowboys' ball cap pulled down over his eyes. Apparently, Jake hadn't returned yet.

Cole sat up and shoved his hat back. He looked much the same as he had years before—light brown hair, blue eyes, tanned and fit. His face had maybe filled out a little, he seemed more mature.

Rachel didn't see Jake's truck anywhere. She climbed out of the van, waved, and got Zoe out of the back.

"Hi, Rachel," Cole said, coming over. "It's great to see you again."

"Hi, Cole." Rachel held out her hand. "I hear congratulations are in order."

He looked at her questioningly.

"I had lunch with Becky the other day."

"Ah, yes. She and Annie are tight." He reached out. "Here, let me help you."

"Thanks." She reached inside, handed him Zoe's diaper bag, and then pointed to the back. "If you could get that playpen."

"Got it," Cole said.

Zoe in her arms, she grabbed the car seat and unlocked Jake's apartment.

"I didn't get a key," Cole said, following her.

Rachel opened the door. "What can I say? Maybe if you were a woman?"

"Maybe." Cole laughed.

Inside, she motioned to the corner. "Could you please set the playpen over there?"

"These things are great," Cole said, studying the unit as he opened it. "I suppose every kid needs one, huh?"

"And lots of other paraphernalia." She placed Zoe inside it. "Why all the interest? You plan on having some kids soon?" Becky had told her Cole was divorced and had been going with a woman named Tessa. Rachel took a couple of toys from the diaper bag and handed them to Zoe.

"I hope so. But I have to get my girlfriend to marry me first."

He looked happy. She hadn't known

him all that well in school, but like most families in River Bluff, their parents knew each other and they'd attended all the same social functions. "I saw your sister earlier today at the newspaper. She seems to be doing well."

Cole beamed. "Yeah. For a change, things seem to be going great for all the Lawrys." He knocked on the wood table.

"I know how you feel," Rachel said. Everything seemed to be working out for her, and she couldn't stop feeling hopeful. The job with Jake was only a wonderful first step. She was grateful to have the chance to make a new life for her and Zoe on her own terms. She had Jake to thank for that.

"So," Cole said, "how's your mother?"

"I haven't had much of a chance to talk to her. She's been gone most of the time since I arrived." She went over, pulled out her portfolio and some drawing paper and sat at the table.

"I heard she's been seeing someone."

She picked at the paper. "So I hear."

Cole gave her a strange look, then cut across the room to the fridge, glanced inside and then closed it again. "I'm going to have to talk to Jake about his beverage situation. It sucks."

Cole sat across from her. "What kind of work are you doing for Jake? He was pretty vague."

"We haven't discussed specifics yet. My training includes structure and design. From knocking down walls to interior decorating." She heard a car. Then she heard voices.

Seconds later, the door opened and Jake came in, his arms full of grocery bags. He dropped them on the table at the same time as a teenager she didn't recognize came in with a few more.

"Hey, Wyatt," Cole said.

"I recruited some help for you," Jake said to Cole.

The kid set the bags on the metal table near the stove.

"Rachel, this is Wyatt. He's going to help wherever he can," Jake said to both

Rachel and Cole. "Cole, can you help me and Wyatt get a few things from the truck?"

Cole followed them outside. Had Jake bought building supplies already? Rachel crossed to the window.

Her mouth dropped open when she saw Cole and Jake trucking a mattress to the side door, hauling it upstairs. The gangly teen followed with the bed rails. In the back of the truck, she saw a couple of boxes. One a microwave oven. The other, she couldn't tell.

She closed her eyes as guilt constricted the muscles in her chest. Jake was doing everything he could to make her comfortable, and she harbored a lie that had changed his life forever. Any day of the week, any minute of any hour, any fraction of a second, he was a better person than she was.

Many times she'd thought about telling him the truth. But he'd moved on. She doubted it would make any difference now. And it could ruin everything for her and Zoe.

She glanced at her little girl, playing happily in the playpen, then she went to the stairwell where the men were laughing. Though she wanted to go up and see what was going on, she decided against it. Just because she was going to work for Jake didn't mean she was a part of his life in any way. His friends were his friends. She was an employee.

In what seemed like only seconds, Zoe had fallen asleep. Rachel didn't know how long they'd take, so she made herself useful and put away the groceries.

Ten minutes later, the three men were finished. "Okay," Jake said. "We're ready to roll." He looked at Zoe. "Maybe we should go into the bar since that's what we're going to be talking about." Rachel took a moment to set up the baby monitor, then stuck the speaker in her pocket.

Jake had cleared off one side of the bar and had retrieved some old bar stools so they could sit. "This is great," she said excitedly. "I can almost feel what it'll be like when it's done."

"Well, let's not get too eager," Jake said. "We're exploring what we want to do, against what we can reasonably do. They're not always the same, and sometimes, even what we think we can reasonably do, isn't an option."

Cole frowned. "That's a crappy attitude."

Jake shook his head. "It's realistic. And because I've got to go to California in a couple of days to take care of some business there, we need to brainstorm now."

THREE HOURS AND two breaks to take care of Zoe later, Jake and Rachel were alone again. She got up from the table where they'd spread all their papers once Zoe had awakened.

"I had someone come in to clean the

apartment this morning, and I fixed a few things. It still needs a lot of work, but it's not as bad as it was. The sink and toilet work, but the tub needs a plumber. In the meantime, you can use the shower downstairs," Jake said.

"Can I go look?"

He stood. "Sure. I'll stay here with Zoe."

Rachel made her way upstairs, grateful to Jake for giving her a job where she could still devote the time necessary to help Zoe.

Developmentally, Zoe was doing better than either the doctor in Chicago or Rachel had expected. It had to be the time she spent with her that made the difference.

Once she got paid, she could get a part-time sitter to watch Zoe while she worked, but Rachel would still be right there.

Reaching the second floor, she flipped on the light. Someone had fixed the chandelier and the place, while not spotless, was relatively clean. The spanking new microwave sat on the kitchen counter. The apartment-size stove was clean, and the bed, with new mattress, was set up in one corner with a large clear plastic bag sitting on top. She read the label. "Bed in a bag. Comforter, two sheets and two pillowcases." Two puffy new pillows lay on top of the bed, as well.

That Jake had thought to do this over-whelmed her. That he'd done it for *her* was even more amazing.

She flopped onto the bed. Glancing around, she thought of all the different things she could do with the place. But as quickly as she thought it, she reminded herself that this was just tem-porary during the time she had the job. Once her work was done, she'd have to leave.

What she didn't understand was why Jake was doing any of this. He didn't want to stay in River Bluff. He'd said so many times. And though he might be helping her because he needed her expertise, he didn't have to be so kind. What was in it for him?

Going downstairs, she heard Jake talking to someone. When she got closer, she saw he was talking to Zoe. Her heart all but melted. When he heard her, he immediately stopped and stood up.

"I should go and get some groceries for upstairs," she said.

He crossed his arms. "Actually, only some of what I bought is for the game tonight. The rest is for you since I knew you'd be working all afternoon. I can take it upstairs right now."

Tears welled in her eyes. She bit her bottom lip to keep it from quivering. Man, she was a mess.

"Why, Jake?"

"Why? Why what?"

"Why are you being so nice to me."

He stiffened. "I'm not being nice to you. I'm protecting my investment. I take care of people who work for me."

That was it then. No big deal. He did this for everyone. She pulled herself up. "Well, then I'm glad to be one of your employees." She tried to smile, but knew it was weak. "I can't thank you enough."

"I don't want your thanks," he said abruptly, then went to the door. "But—" he turned "—if you wanted to make dinner, I wouldn't object."

Her smile returned. "I'd love to."

A knock on the door interrupted them. Jake answered and saw it was Wyatt. He'd assumed the kid had left with Cole.

"You wanted me to clear a spot for the building materials, but I'm not finished yet," Wyatt said. "I'll come back tomorrow if that's okay?"

Jake went out with him and closed the door behind them. He'd been surprised in town when he saw Wyatt and the kid had asked for a job. "Looks okay to me. There's no need to come back." He shoved a hand into his pocket and pulled out some bills.

"No, don't pay me yet. I want to finish." He stuck out his chin. "I want to do a good job."

"Any particular reason you think it isn't good?"

"I didn't finish. I need to finish what I started."

Jake put his money away. The kid was needy, that was obvious. "Okay. Come back tomorrow and finish."

Wyatt started to go.

"Come to think of it," Jake said. "Cole can use an extra hand, too." Cole *had* mentioned something about needing a gopher to speed things up.

Turning, the teen's face lit up like Kleg lights at a nighttime rodeo. "Give me a chance, I can do so much more for you around here."

Jake buried a grin. "I'm sure you can. I'll let you know tomorrow."

"Okay, Mr. Chandler. Than—"

He held up a hand. "No thanks. You work, I'll pay. Now scram."

Watching Wyatt get in his GTO and

pull away, Jake felt an odd kinship with the teen.

"Dinner is almost ready," Rachel said, peering out the door.

He turned and walked back inside. "Do I have time for a shower?"

"Just," she said. "Ten minutes."

"Good." Jake went into the bedroom. As he undressed, he thought about Rachel—the girl who'd once filled his fantasies—and who he'd hated for even longer. Rachel, who was now in his kitchen cooking dinner for them. Indeed, the cliché was true. Business made for strange bedfellows.

Thank God he had a poker game tonight.

"WHERE HAVE YOU BEEN, WYATT? I was worried about you." Wade studied his son, who seemed distant, even more so than usual. And his clothes were filthy.

"Hanging out down by the river."

"Well, next time let me know where you are. That's why I bought you a cell phone."

"I'm sorry. I forgot and left it in my room."

"Well, don't forget again."

"I won't."

Wade was glad the teen was finally talking to him. He'd made such a mess of raising Kyle, his firstborn, that he'd tried hard to do things right with Wyatt. His older son had moved away one year out of high school, so Wyatt had grown up almost like an only child. A task Wade had never felt up for—especially after how Kyle had turned on him. And now, God knew, he wasn't as young as he used to be.

"Why don't you get together with Shane Howard?" Wade said. "He's a nice guy."

"I don't even know him. And it's hard to make friends when I just have to go back to school again in two weeks. Why can't I stay here like other kids?"

Wyatt's mom came into the room. Ellie walked over and hugged Wyatt, then kissed Wade.

"I don't like it that you have to go, either, sweetheart. But—" she looked at Wade "—we think it's best."

Wade felt the strain between them. His wife didn't think it was best. He wasn't sure he did anymore, either, since the military school hadn't changed his son's nature. He was still shy and withdrawn.

"Maybe we can think about it this summer," Ellie said, smiling at Wade. "Well, it's almost time for dinner." Her gaze drifted over the boy. "How did you get so dirty anyway?"

"I—I fell off my bike."

"Well, go clean up," his mother said.

Wade had an odd feeling that the teen wasn't telling the truth. Lately he'd been even more quiet, more secretive, going off and not saying where he'd been. Ellie protected him too much. He needed to have a long talk with Wyatt.

One of these days.

## CHAPTER ELEVEN

JAKE HAD WORRIED that Rachel wouldn't get out of there before the guys arrived for the game. But she'd finally managed, saying she still had a room at the motel for the night. He had enough to think about without worrying whether they made too much noise for the baby.

Harold was the first to show. He shoved a bottle of wine into Jake's hand. "That's from Sally."

Jake could tell from his tone that Harold was in a mood. "Tell her thanks. Did she say what it's for?"

"A housewarming thing or something like that."

"Ah. Well, tell her she's very thoughtful."

"Yeah, maybe she is sometimes." He walked through the room, scanning it. "I'll be damned glad when you get this place fixed up, Chandler."

The word was out. He should've figured that. And he should've known why Harold was in such a cranky mood. In the short time Jake had been back, he'd already deciphered that Harold's mood hinged on whether he and Sally were fighting or not. "I can see you got a bug up your butt, Harry, but don't take it out on me."

Harry shoved a chair out of the way. "It's Sally. She's been nagging me to get one of them tests that she says every guy should have. I told her no one's going to be poking on parts I've reserved specially for her."

Jake laughed, but before he could respond, the door was flung open and Cole and Blake came in together. Jake gave them the job of putting leaves in the table, and as they finished, Ed Falconetti arrived.

"Something smells good," Jake said.

"Hamburgers from the Longhorn, and

if we don't eat them now, they'll get cold."

"Jake's got a brand-new microwave upstairs," Cole said. "One zap and they'll be hot again."

"Upstairs?" Luke, Harold and Ed said almost simultaneously.

"What the hell for?" Harold snapped.

All eyes went to Jake, who shot Cole an evil look. Hell, they'd all know sooner or later, anyway. "I'm renting out the apartment."

Just then Brady and his dad, Marshall Carrick, came in. "Renting out what?" Brady asked.

"The upstairs," Harold answered.

"I hope it looks better than this place," Marshall said. "We should've played at Cross Fox."

Brady walked over to the table and sat at the end. "No, we shouldn't," he said, directing his gaze at Jake. "This place is a historic landmark. We've played here longest and so did a lot of other people. If we can get Jake to stay—"

"So, who's the renter?" Marshall interrupted. "I didn't know anyone in town was looking for a place."

Cole, Harold, Ed and Luke turned to Jake again.

He cleared his throat. "I've hired a designer. She'll be using the upstairs while she's working here," he mumbled. It got so quiet, he could hear himself breathe. "It's easier that way because she has a kid," he added quickly.

The rest of the guys gathered at the table in their usual seats. Jake picked up the silver case with the cards and chips and sat to open it. When he did, he heard the click of metal against metal echo through the room. "Let's get this game started."

"Wait a minute," Brady said, as if the news had just sunk in. "You're going to renovate?"

Jake smiled and reached for a handful of poker chips. "That's the rumor."

"Damn," Blake chimed in. "Annie

asked me, but I denied it. Now I'm going to have to admit I was wrong."

"Hey, a guy can be wrong once in a while," Cole needled his brother-in-law. "Especially when he's got a wife driving him crazy with cravings."

The door opened and Trevor Dobbs came in. "Don't start without me." Dobbs worked at Cross Fox Ranch and mostly stayed to himself. But the guy loved poker and was there every chance he could get. He pulled up a chair. "Still fifty bucks buy-in?"

"Fifty bucks and another twenty for one of Ed's hamburgers," Luke said.

"I thought I smelled something rotten. I'm glad I ate before I came."

"What's there to drink?" Luke asked, taking off his hat to shove his hair back with one hand. Then he placed the hat back on again. Good. Luke was easier to read with his hat on.

"Whatever you want," Jake said, tipping his head toward the kitchen. "As long as what you want is beer."

While Jake handed out chips, Cole gathered the buy-in. "Hoo, yeah," he said. "I like tournament play. We've got two-fifty for first place, one-fifty for second and third gets his buy-in back. I could use the win. I'm headed back to Oregon after we get this renovation stuff started."

Feeling a moment of panic, Jake looked at Cole. He couldn't manage without Cole. Well, maybe he could, but he didn't want to.

"Relax," Cole added. "It's only for a day or two. When Tessa is ready, I'm going to help her drive that U-Haul back."

Jake felt a wave of relief. Just then, Marshall got up and headed for the door.

"Set me up. I'll be right back. Got a business call to make."

Jake had wondered what kind of response he'd get about his decision. Not so much from his buddies, but from people like Marshall Carrick. His generation had played at the Wild Card in its heyday.

If Jake knew anything at all, he knew Marshall was on the phone with Barstow this very minute.

"Okay," Jake said. "Let's get this game started."

LATE THE NEXT DAY, Jake pulled into the driveway at the Wild Card, tired from lack of sleep the night before. He didn't see Rachel's van. He'd gone to San Antonio early this morning, but he'd left a message for her at the motel that he might not be back when she got here.

He'd applied for a building permit and was told it would take a few days, so he'd bought supplies that he figured he'd need to start, ordered some of the things he had on his list from the meeting with Cole and Rachel yesterday, and now, even though it was almost evening, he was ready to get started.

He saw movement in the yard and Wyatt appeared from the shadows.

"Hey, nice ride," the young man said, crossing to Jake.

Jake stepped out of the almost new Dodge Dakota Club Cab he'd purchased in San Antonio. He'd be hauling a lot of building supplies and he doubted the old pickup he'd bought from Hap would last much longer. "It'll serve the purpose."

"You trade in the old one?"

"Yep. It wasn't going to last much longer."

"I finished cleaning up."

As the teen turned to go, Jake asked, "Did Rachel say where she was going or when she'd be back?"

He shook his head.

"Okay. Thanks."

Wyatt leapt into his GTO and took off.

Man, Jake felt like an idiot. He wasn't Rachel's keeper. They'd agreed that she'd work a normal schedule, unless her daughter required care. It hadn't occurred to him that he'd look forward to her being here, or wonder where she was when she wasn't here.

As Jake turned to go inside, he saw something smoldering near his Harley.

He walked over, bent down and held his hand over the mound. Still hot. Odd. What reason would Wyatt have for making a fire? If he was cold, he should've gone home earlier. Jake shook his head.

A half hour later, working in the bar, Jake heard a car and went to the window. Rachel's van pulled into the drive, and he felt a quick twist of relief. He put down his hammer and went outside. "Need some help?"

"I'm good. But thanks anyway."

She gave him the once-over.

"It's dirty work," he said. "I put up some plastic sheeting over the doorway to keep the dust from going upstairs. How'd everything go today?"

Placing Zoe on her hip, Rachel gave the child a kiss. "Everything went well. I made some rough sketches and put together a couple of idea packets." Smiling, she said, "I think you'll like them."

Her face seemed to glow and he could

tell how much she enjoyed her work. "I'll take a look later."

"It's better if we do it together. I'll have to explain some things."

"Okay. Whenever you're ready." He'd rather do it right now, but he was the one who'd made her say she'd stick to the hours they decided. He didn't want her working all hours as he sometimes did.

He liked the idea of sitting down with her, going over plans. Again he was reminded of when he'd started his company—the uncertainty, anticipation…and the seemingly impossible hope that it would work. Good feelings to have. Made him feel alive again.

"Oh, Wade Barstow's attorney called earlier," Rachel said. "Something about an easement on the property and that he'd call back another time."

Jake clenched his hands. Barstow just didn't give up.

RACHEL TOOK ZOE INSIDE, unsure if she'd done the right thing by not telling Jake what she'd heard in town. But he couldn't do anything about it, so what was the point?

She turned on the light and went upstairs. After exercises with Zoe, dinner and bathing her in the sink, her little girl was ready for bed. "You like your new home, don't you, sweetie?"

Zoe nestled her head against Rachel's shoulder, almost as if she understood. She smelled baby fresh and Rachel loved her so much her chest ached. Once tucked into bed, Zoe dropped right off to sleep. Rachel stood for a moment watching her.

For the first time in months, she finally felt as if she'd be able to give her little girl the life she deserved.

Today, while Jake was gone, Rachel had created a bedroom for Zoe in one corner—the farthest from the construction—by using some of the leftover fabric she'd brought along from past jobs. With a few nails, hinges and some plywood she'd found in a shed out back, she'd covered the wood with red fabric and had a nice room divider. On the other side, she'd pieced together some fabric scraps to make a curtain of red and gold, strung it on some wire she'd found and, voilà. She'd tied one side back with a ribbon and decided the effect was quite nice. Hobo chic, she'd call it.

Once she was sure Zoe was sound asleep, she strode to the round barrel chair that seemed like something from an old fifties sitcom, and plunked down in it. Looking out the picture window, which she'd draped with another piece of red fabric to give her privacy, she pulled out her cell phone and punched in her mother's number.

After ringing five times, the answering machine came on. Rachel waited until she heard the beep. "Mother, it's Rachel. I need to talk to you as soon as possible. Please call me. It's very important." She left her number and closed the phone. Even though her mother wanted nothing to do with her, she needed to let her know where they were and how they were doing. She still wished things could be different between them.

She heard a noise outside, then lifted the curtain on one side to peer out. A waning crescent moon shone above her, and with the yard light on, she saw a man's form moving in the shadows. She couldn't be sure, but she didn't believe it was Jake.

Quickly she turned on the baby monitor in Zoe's room, put the battery unit in her pocket, and went downstairs, where she heard Jake pounding as he worked. "Jake," she said, pulling aside the plastic sheet he'd hung over the doorway.

He stood hunched over behind the bar, doing something with a crowbar. He looked up. "Yeah, what?"

He wore a bandana over his longish hair and his sleeveless shirt was unbuttoned in the front exposing ripples she'd only imagined before now. "I was sitting by the window upstairs and saw some-one in the yard."

He dropped the crowbar immediately. "Where's Zoe?"

"She's sleeping. I have the monitor." She touched her pocket.

"Where did you see—this person?"

"In back, near the trees."

He grabbed the crowbar, turned and rushed out the side door. What if he got hurt? But she couldn't follow him with Zoe upstairs.

She shut the door and locked it, then went into Jake's apartment and found his cell phone on the table. Holding it in her hand ready to call 911, she peered out the kitchen window. Jake had flipped on the yard lights and she saw him looking first by the trees, then in the shed and then the truck bed. He scratched his head as he came back into the kitchen.

"Everything okay?" she asked.

"I think so, but it's hard to tell."

"Maybe I was imagining things?"

He looked at her, his eyebrows raised.

"Would you have come downstairs if you thought you were imagining things?"

She shook her head. "Maybe someone was lost?"

"Yeah, they'd have to be, out here at this time of night."

She felt chilled suddenly, and her hands shook. She was more scared than she realized. She placed both hands against her cheeks. "I guess I should go back upstairs."

"Are you okay?"

"Just a little shook up."

He reached out and pulled her into his arms as if it was the most natural thing in the world.

"Maybe a glass of wine will soothe your nerves."

As far as she was concerned, standing here with his arms around her was more soothing than a glass of wine could ever be. "That sounds good."

He pushed back, gave her a quick friendly pat, then opened the fridge.

"Nothing fancy, just a bottle of chardonnay one of the guys brought over last night."

"Wine at a poker game?"

"Sally sent it with Harold."

"That was nice of her."

He got out two glasses, found a corkscrew to open it, then poured them each a half glass. She raised her glass to his. "Here's to a successful renovation."

His expression seemed to soften as he clinked his glass against hers. "To success, whatever that may be."

They sipped together and then just stood there, his gaze never leaving hers.

She felt like an amoeba under a microscope. "What are your plans once the bar is finished? Will you stay and run the place?"

He scowled. "I'd never live here again."

"Then why renovate?"

A wicked smile curled his lips. "Because I can."

"And why hire me?"

His expression became shuttered. "You needed a job. I need someone to do a job."

"Everything you've done is more than I'd have expected." She pursed her lips. "Considering."

"One might think that," he said, edging closer until he was standing mere inches from her, so close she could feel his body heat. "Or, one might think I have other motives."

Her heartbeat quickened. He didn't mean… Oddly, the idea aroused her. Made her pulse race. She pulled herself up. "Do you—" her breathing became heavy and suddenly she didn't give a damn and she wanted to kiss him in the worst way "—have other motives?"

His gaze had locked on her mouth, and he seemed to be inching closer. Or was she the one moving closer? Did it even matter? She leaned forward and kissed him, soft at first, then quickly she brought her arms around his neck, deepening the kiss with a passion she didn't know she had in her. His lips still on hers, he embraced her, almost lifting her off her feet as he kissed her back as passionately as she was kissing him.

She felt his shoulder muscles under her fingers, his hard body pressed against hers, his obvious need.

She wanted to touch him, all of him. But just as her hands dropped lower on his back, he pulled away.

Her lips throbbed.

"This is a really bad idea," he said, his breathing labored.

"Oh, no," she said, her voice sounding husky and not her own. "It's a wonderful idea."

He dropped his arms and took a step back. "Uh—as nice as that was, it wasn't my motivation for hiring you."

Her face warmed. Was that sarcasm? No. She'd seen the heat in his eyes, seen his awareness of her. She walked slowly around him, picked up the bottle and poured more wine in her glass. She took a slow sip and looked directly into his eyes. "No? You could've hired any number of people with my skills."

A slow smile lifted the corners of his mouth.

"Maybe you only *think* you hired me for my skills—and other altruistic reasons," she continued. "Helping a woman with a baby and all that."

He dragged his gaze from her head to her toes, then back again. He crossed his arms. "Or maybe I hired you because you were always so unattainable and now *you* need *me*."

Rachel's throat closed. She couldn't breathe. He'd hired her to get even?

She wanted to lash out, to say something to hurt him back, but she couldn't. Instead, deliberately she set down her glass, turned and left the room.

THE NEXT DAY, as Rachel sat at the big table near the window in the upstairs apartment, she pondered the sketches she'd made for the renovations. She liked three of the ideas equally, but ultimately, Jake would decide. There were many things to do before the actual renovation started. The place had structural issues, so first came the demolition, then rebuilding. Decorating was last.

But try as she might to get her head into the project, she kept coming back to last night. She'd lost sleep over it.

Well, she had what she wanted for at least three or four months, she had a job and a place to live. She'd do what she needed to, and when the work was finished, she'd have money to move on, and hopefully, set up shop in her own place.

All love ever got her was another person who wanted to control her life. Another person to let her know she wasn't perfect.

If Jake wanted her expertise, he'd get the best she had. He'd get what he paid for and she wouldn't feel beholden to anyone for anything. What Jake thought of her didn't matter. What mattered was what she thought of herself.

She shoved back the papers in front of her, unable to convince herself that it didn't matter. The reality was that she'd always feel guilty for what she'd done to Jake. There was no fix for it. She deserved the humiliation.

The worst part was that even if she told him the truth, she couldn't change how her lie had affected his life.

But…she could help. After all, her mother was trying to prevent Jake from reopening the Wild Card. The woman could make things difficult for him. Or at least take some of the joy out of the project. Surely in this day and age, self-righteous zealots didn't have the power to sway a community against the evils of alcohol and gambling. It was absurd. *Wasn't* it?

She'd have to talk to her mother and stop this nonsense now. But her mother had never listened to Rachel before, what made her think she would now?

Not talking to her was taking the easy way out. Hiding her head in the sand.

And if Jake couldn't renovate, as difficult as that was to believe—the town had other bars, for goodness' sake—she'd be out of a job. A selfish reason, but there it was. She had to talk to her mother. But not over the phone.

She looked over at Zoe who was taking time waking up from her morning nap, tossing and gurgling, but refusing to open her eyes. Jake was gone, getting more supplies and Cole was downstairs sanding the rest of the floor Jake had started last night. Cole had other workers coming to help tomorrow. Wyatt had been enlisted as well, and the young man seemed excited about it.

"Hello there, punkin," Rachel said when Zoe finally raised her eyelids. She loved how Zoe always woke up happy, and could only hope she always would.

She heard a vehicle outside, picked up Zoe and went to the window. Jake had returned. She didn't know how she was going to face him again.

JAKE TRIED NOT TO watch Rachel as she packed up her van to leave. She'd barely said a word to him.

He couldn't blame her for being angry. What he'd done was inexcusable. The worst part was that he didn't know if he'd done it to get even, or to protect himself from getting involved. Lord knew, he wanted to.

So now she hated him and he didn't have to worry about doing something he'd regret later.

"How'd it go?" Cole asked when Jake went into the bar to see how he was doing with the demo.

"Still no word on the building permit."

"It's only been two days."

"Yeah, yeah. I know. But we can only go so far without it."

"Look, I've got to take off for an hour or so," Cole said. "I have to pick up a few things." Jake knew Cole was planning for Tessa to move in with him, and he wanted his own place done before she came back.

Out of the window, Jake saw Wyatt

walking over to Jake's bike. "Sure. No problem. By the way, how's Wyatt doing? Following your instructions?"

Cole shrugged. "Sometimes he seems a little spacey, but he's doing fine. I'm surprised you hired him."

Jake frowned. "Why wouldn't I?"

"You don't *know?*"

"Know what?"

"Wyatt is Wade Barstow's youngest kid."

Jake fisted his hands. "No, I didn't." But he wished he had. He turned to leave. "No big deal."

He wondered if Barstow knew his kid was working for Jake. Or had Barstow sent him here to spy?

"Okay," Cole said. "I'm outta here. I'll be back soon."

Jake followed Cole out the door, then strode over to where Wyatt was still standing by Jake's Harley. "It's nice, isn't it?" Jake said.

The young man nodded. "It's awesome. Some day I'm going to have one just like it."

Jake kicked a rock with the tip of his boot. "You'll have to earn a lot more than I'm paying you," he said, joking to take the edge off how he felt right now. "Maybe your parents can buy you one?"

Wyatt shook his head.

"My par—my mom…she'd never do that."

"How about your dad?" Jake pressed to see how far the kid would go.

Wyatt looked away, sweat beading on his forehead even though it was cold. "I…told you he—"

"Come to think of it," Jake said as he planted his feet apart in an authoritative stance. "I've been in town for five weeks now. How come I never saw you around before last week?"

"I go to military school in Austin. I'm only home for four weeks on vacation."

"I see. Well, maybe you can save your money and get a secondhand bike by the end of the summer. I had one when I was sixteen."

Wyatt shook his head. "No, my dad would never allow me to have one. Trusts me with his GTO, but not a two-wheeler."

"Well, you know what, if I had a sixteen-year-old kid, I wouldn't let him, either. Regardless of my own experience."

Wyatt's face fell. "That doesn't make sense."

"A motorcycle got me nothin' but trouble back then. Take my word for it. Don't get into trouble. It won't help anything."

"Maybe you could let me borrow yours."

Jake looked at Wyatt, searching for some common physical trait. He didn't see any. "Not a chance. The only way I'd let you ride it is if your parents approved. And then you'd have to have training. Without training, you could get hurt."

Wyatt looked at Jake and for the first time, Jake saw that his eyes were red, his pupils dilated. Telltale signs of drug abuse. Was that why he'd avoided looking at Jake? "Do your parents even know you're doing work for me?"

Wyatt shook his head. "No, and I don't want them to. They'd make me quit."

"Yeah?" Jake felt a quick surge of adrenaline. "Why would they do that?"

Wyatt looked away, obviously embarrassed to say. Jake could imagine. Jake might be a bad influence. Well, he had news. From the look of his eyes, Wyatt was already into something he probably couldn't handle.

"Okay," Jake said. "We both better get to work or this place isn't going to get done."

Inside, Jake slammed his hand on the table, wondering how he could've missed this little Barstow tidbit. Why hadn't anyone said anything to him before? Rachel…did she know? She had to. Had Wyatt heard the old rumors? He didn't seem to. But then, maybe he thought Jake would fire him if he knew.

Dammit. He went to the fridge for a soda, then to the table where Rachel's drawings were spread out. Why would the kid be doing scut work for Jake when his dad had more money than anyone in the county? He fingered the drawings.

If the rumors were true, Wyatt would be Jake's half brother.

## *CHAPTER TWELVE*

JAKE TOOK ANOTHER SWIPE at the bar with the sander. It was hard to get all the gouges out without taking it down too far. Rachel, on the other side of the room examining the chandelier, had suggested that the marks gave the bar character. He agreed and had limited his sanding to the worst spots.

It had been a week since he last checked on the building permit and liquor license, and still, he'd heard nothing. Something was holding things up and he needed to find out exactly what it was. Only it was Saturday and everyone was gone, including Cole and the guys working for him. Wyatt had come around, but Jake had told him to take the day off.

They were almost to the point to move ahead with the new windows and the addition to create a separate area for a stage and dance floor.

He'd loved Rachel's idea to make the pecan grove usable for special events. Jake and Rachel had developed a solid, professional working relationship, and even Zoe seemed to take to him. At least she smiled and babbled at him every time he stopped to talk to her.

Rachel held something up to the light, and he slowed his sanding. She was the ultimate professional when it came to her craft, and she demanded perfection from herself. He wondered if she ever cut herself an inch of slack.

He wasn't all that different in the perfection category, but he knew how to step back when necessary. He had outlets. Poker for one. She didn't seem to have any. When she wasn't working, she was a patient and loving mother, giving and protective. In fact, except for the one time when she'd had Becky watch Zoe, she hadn't been away from her daughter the whole time they'd been working. Yet she never complained.

For the first time, he realized he was seeing the real Rachel. And he had to admit, the real Rachel was wonderful.

"Jake," Rachel said, still preoccupied with the chandelier. "I'm going to take a run into San Antonio. Do you want me to pick up anything for you?"

"When are you going?"

"As soon as Zoe wakes up."

"Why don't you go and I'll listen for her?"

She glanced at him, eyes wide.

"What? You don't think I'd hear her?"

She moistened her lips, frowning. "No, I'm sure you would. She's quite vocal when she wants to be. But would you know what to do with her when she's awake?"

He shrugged. "Sure. I've been around kids before. You pick them up when they cry, feed them or change them or play with them."

"Well—" she said, her voice skeptical.

"Look, a buddy of mine in California had three kids. He stayed with me for a while after his wife died. I sat with all three kids several times. I'm a seriously good babysitter. Trust me."

"But—"

"No buts. You've been working constantly, except when you're taking care of Zoe, and you haven't been by yourself in what—two weeks? Everyone needs some downtime."

"I get that time when she's sleeping."

He narrowed his eyes. "It's not the same."

"I suppose you're right." She hesitated. "Are you sure?"

He raised an eyebrow.

"Okay— I should be back before she needs to eat, and there's some juice in the—"

"Just give me the monitor and go already."

When Rachel left, he placed the monitor on the bar and continued sanding. He couldn't help smiling. She trusted him with her daughter, and it felt good.

A half hour later, he heard a knock on the door. He wasn't expecting anyone and when he looked at the car—a big tan Mercedes—he didn't recognize it.

He shoved a hand through his hair, took off his carpenter's apron and grabbed the monitor before going to the door.

He opened it before there was a second knock and when he did, a strong breeze could've knocked him over.

"Mrs. Diamonte!" His surprise was surpassed only by his irritation when she pushed past him.

"Where's Rachel? I need to talk to her." She swung around, her gaze zeroed in on his ragged jeans with holes in each knee.

He managed to close his mouth before saying, "She's not here."

"Fine. I can say what I have to to you as easily as to her."

He motioned to a chair at the kitchen

table, but she shook her head. "This won't take long."

"You won't mind if I sit, will you?" he sat and crossed his arms. "What's on your mind?"

"My daughter and granddaughter," she huffed. "Rachel sent me a letter telling me how she wants things to be different between us. But if she wants that, she'll have to give up this ridiculous job."

Ridiculous job. A letter? He was curious, he had to say. Rachel hadn't told him anything about what was going on between her and her mother, but he'd known there was something.

"A bar is no place to raise children. Rachel is not thinking of what's best for her child and I want her to leave here immediately."

It took all the willpower he had not to tell her to get the hell out of there. "That's something you need to take up with Rachel, not me. I'm only her employer."

"That's not what people are saying."

"Oh? And what are people saying?"

"Use your imagination."

"I can imagine all kinds of things, but I doubt anything would come close to what you have in mind."

She pulled back as if she'd been slapped. Then she fished a piece of paper out of her handbag.

"This place was a black mark on the town back when your mother was running it, but we've had a clean town ever since it closed down. No gambling, no rowdy partying. The people who signed this petition don't want your kind of establishment in this town. A bar of this sort draws all the unsavory elements that we want to keep out of River Bluff."

"Are you the spokesperson for this— coalition?"

She lifted her chin. "I am in this case."

"Ah, I see. I guess I'm wondering how you know what kind of bar this is going to be, when I don't even know yet. In fact, that's one of the things Rachel and I are working on."

He had a feeling he should be nice to her, that he should be making friends, not enemies, but when she attacked Rachel, he saw fire.

Just then, Jake heard a tiny cry through the monitor.

"Is that the baby?"

Jake stood. "Zoe is upstairs. She was sleeping until this minute."

"Rachel's gone and she left her child here with you?"

Jake motioned to the door. "I think we're done here."

Mrs. Diamonte set her jaw. "We aren't done. I would like to see the baby. I want to know that she's okay."

Jake looked at her. She *was* the child's grandmother.

Suddenly the woman moved like a rabbit, dashed into the hall and up the stairs, as if she knew exactly where to go. Jake followed on her heels.

Mrs. Diamonte found the little

bedroom Rachel had made, but Jake grabbed her arm just before she went in. He pulled her back and whispered as firmly as he could, "I'm taking care of her while Rachel's gone."

"Do you think I care about that?" she snapped, storming into the room. "She's already done enough to destroy my reputation. I'll get a court order and take this child away from her if she persists in staying here with you."

As if on cue, Zoe started crying harder.

Mrs. Diamonte pulled back.

Jake glared at the woman. "You're her grandmother. Go ahead and pick her up."

Zoe wailed. Mrs. Diamonte edged away. "What's wrong with her?"

"Absolutely nothing," Jake said, reaching down. "It's okay, kiddo," he said soothingly as he lifted the baby from the crib. She stopped crying instantly. "Did you get scared by all the loud talking?"

Mrs. Diamonte seemed frozen in place, so he said, "She was just surprised by the noise. Would you like to hold her?" Zoe gurgled.

"What's wrong with her eyes?"

Hearing the door, Jake turned and said sharply, "There's nothing wrong."

Rachel, who'd arrived none too soon, came in and took Zoe from him. "She's perfect. Absolutely perfect."

"Rachel," the older woman said sternly. "I need to talk with you privately."

Jake saw Rachel flinch. "We can talk right here, Mother."

The woman went stiff as a pole. She pulled her handbag to her chest. "I received your letter and I'd like to talk to you. If you and the child will come with me, I can make room for you at my house where your baby can get a proper upbringing."

Fire ignited in Rachel's eyes. But her words were calm. Even. "A proper upbringing? Like the one I had? Please,

Mother. I came back because I was desperate. I had no place else to go. And you rejected me."

Rachel's eyes glistened with tears and Jake wanted to put his arms around her. Protect her.

"Even then, I thought maybe if we could talk, maybe we could find some way back to each other. That's why I wrote the letter. But now—" Rachel's mouth quivered "—now—that's the last thing I want. Not for me or for my daughter, whose name is Zoe by the way." Rachel turned and walked to the window.

Mrs. Diamonte's face paled, then she looked confused, as if she didn't know what to do. Jake almost felt sorry for her. Caught between them, he looked at Rachel, hoping for a clue. "Rachel?"

She turned. "Thanks for watching her, Jake. I've got some things for you to look at after my mother leaves." She nailed her mother with a look that could've wilted steel.

Mrs. Diamonte took a breath, squared her shoulders, then walked to the stairs. "All I want to do is help you, Rachel. But I don't think you'll ever learn. Now, again, you've made your bed and you'll have to lie in it."

Rachel clutched Zoe a little tighter, apparently trying to keep her emotions in check. After a long moment staring out the window, she asked quietly, "Is she gone?"

"She is."

Calmly, she walked over for a diaper and then laid Zoe on the bed. "Well, wasn't that fun?" she said, more to herself than to him.

Jake said, "I'm confused. Did you know she felt that way?"

"I've always known how she felt about everything. From the time I could walk, she let me know exactly what I could and couldn't do. What I should do. Everything had to have her approval. And I mean everything."

He didn't respond, so she went on. "My mother believes perfection is next to

Godliness." She paused. "No, wait, I take that back. She thinks perfection *is* Godliness. And she expected her family to be perfect. Once I went off to college, I realized I could never be what she wanted me to be, though it wasn't for lack of trying."

Jake nodded his understanding. "What about your father? He seemed like a nice guy. I saw him several times right here when I was a kid."

"Hence her vendetta against the Wild Card. She was convinced he wouldn't have strayed if he hadn't come here."

Jake dropped onto the bed and held his hands up for Zoe to grab on and pull herself up. "No wonder she hated my mother." He shook his head. "My mother had faults, but she wasn't as bad as everyone thought."

Her expression softened. "Well, my mother isn't like everyone believes she is, either. Her marriage was a sham, our happy family was a sham. Her whole life is about how things look to others."

She sighed. "I got married to get away from it. I wanted a real marriage, a happy home, security, a big family—Unfortunately I married someone just like her. Maybe I knew that subconsciously. I don't know. After my dad died, knowing how she treated him, I couldn't bring myself to see her."

"She did say she wanted to help you now."

She took over, lifting Zoe up and down, exercises to strengthen her legs. "Right. She wants to help me so she can control me."

After a moment, Rachel added, "She did the same thing before. When I got pregnant—unexpectedly. That's when I found out Alex and I didn't want the same things. And then I found out Zoe had Down syndrome. Alex saw it as the ideal excuse for me to get an abortion. And my mother was appalled when I didn't. The marriage failed. My mother told me I was paying the price."

She wiped Zoe's mouth with a tissue.

"I didn't talk to her after that. Except once—when she rejected me again."

"So, why did you come back?"

She took a long breath. "I was desperate."

Jake didn't know what to say. He never imagined she'd had problems growing up. "You have the love of a beautiful, happy child and your mother and ex have nothing that could equal that. Not even close."

Tears fell on her cheeks and she pulled Zoe into her arms. He reached over and hugged them both, and held on until he felt her stop crying.

"Oh, boy," she said, moving away. "You never signed on for something like this when you hired me. I'm sorry I fell apart."

She was sorry. He held her at arm's length. "Don't ever apologize for your feelings."

She managed a limp smile and nodded.

Unable to contain all the emotions

coursing through him, he had to get out. If he didn't, he might do something truly stupid. "Will you be okay?"

"I'll be fine," she said softly. "More than fine."

He went to the stairwell and started down.

"Jake."

He stopped.

"Thank you."

RACHEL HAD JUST FINISHED showering when she heard the distant sound of Jake's motorcycle. It was late, but she'd been unable to sleep. All she could think about was the earlier incident with her mother…and how lovingly Jake had held her in his arms. She'd wanted to stay like that all night.

She finished toweling off, put on her nightshirt, then stuck her feet into her fuzzy slippers, hoping to make a cup of cocoa and get back upstairs before Jake came in. But she was too late.

The door swung open. Seeing her,

Jake stopped in his tracks, his hair wind-blown, his face flushed from the cold. "Are you okay?" he asked, shutting the door.

She reached for her robe and, putting it on, said, "I'm fine. I was about to make a cup of cocoa. You look cold. Would you like one, too?"

He shrugged off his leather jacket. "I'd love one. It's starting to rain and that makes it feel even colder outside. Especially on a bike."

"I always hated cold rain. At least in Chicago it turned into snow."

"And according to the song, it never rains in southern California. It pours." He smiled, hung up his jacket on an old hall tree near the door, then sat at the table.

He pulled one of her sketches toward him. She got another mug and mixed two mugs of cocoa, and microwaved them for two minutes.

As she set the steaming hot chocolate down on the table, he placed a hand on her arm.

"Are you sure you're okay?"

"I'm fine." Except that his touch ignited a desire inside her that was hard to ignore.

"Cheers," he said, reaching over to touch her cup with his, catching her eye. Simultaneously they lifted their cups to drink. She watched the muscles in his throat work as he swallowed.

He watched her, too, and she couldn't help feeling as if something had changed between them.

God knew, she'd never intended to lay all her past problems out there for him to see, but now she sensed that it might've brought them closer. She liked that feeling. But even more, she liked the feeling she'd had when he held her in his arms so protectively.

She sipped slowly, acutely aware that the warmth of the cocoa wasn't the only thing that was making her feel so hot. She licked the sweet chocolate from her lips. "Perfect," she said.

He smiled. "Yes, perfect."

"When was the last time you came back to River Bluff to see your uncle?"

"Where did that come from?"

She placed both hands around her cup, warming them, more because she was self-conscious than cold. "I don't know. I was just wondering how close you were. What it might have been like to grow up without anyone telling you what to do and how to do it all the time."

He looked into his mug.

"I always envied the freedom you and your friends had," she added. "I would've given anything to be just a little bit wild."

He took another sip. "I would've given anything if my mother had been here to tell me what to do every second of every day."

Oh, Lord. "I'm sorry," she said. "I didn't mean—I guess that was the wrong way to put it."

He laid a hand over hers. "It's okay. But not having anyone give a damn about what you do can be awful. And when you make mistakes and everyone tells you you're something you're not, it's tough to know who you really are."

He hauled in a lungful of air, his chest expanding. "Kids need guidance, someone who can give direction."

Rain beat on the tin roof above them. He directed his gaze a little beyond her. "We all envy what we don't have. In the end, we all have to find our own way."

"And do you think you've found yours?"

Straightening his legs, he leaned on one elbow. "I think so. I took care of my mother the last year before she died and when Verne moved in, I took care of him because he was drunk all the time. I didn't see that as having freedom. I didn't have freedom until I left River Bluff. Then I had no responsibilities to anyone but myself. It was a great feeling."

Was that why he'd never married? She felt even more self-conscious. "It's funny. I guess neither one of us was the person everyone thought we were back then."

"You turned out all right, though," he said, his voice soft and low, his eyes warming her. He reached to touch her hand. "Very all right."

She swallowed, her mouth dry. "You, too. Very all right." The way he was looking at her made her pulse quicken and she wanted to lean over and kiss him. Instead, she stood to take the cups to the sink. As she picked up his mug, he stood, too, then took the cup out of her hand and set it back on the table.

Then he leaned down to kiss her, his lips touching hers ever so lightly. Soft. Sensual. He tasted of cocoa.

She inhaled deeply, kissing him back, tentative at first. Then getting braver, she explored his mouth with her tongue. She'd never known kissing could be so erotic. If she'd ever had a reason for resisting, she'd lost all sight of it.

Her arms were no longer at her sides but around his neck. Then sliding her hands down, she explored the hard muscled ridges on his back under his shirt with her fingers. And then his chest—she'd dreamed of touching his chest. Desire spiraled through her, and she felt as if her senses might spin out of control.

Ever so tenderly, he kissed the tip of her chin, her jaw, her neck, her lips, then dragged a slow-burning trail of kisses down to the soft hollow at the base of her throat.

She tipped her head back. A low moan escaped her as he bent to kiss her breasts through the soft cotton of her shirt. His breath was moist and hot through the fabric.

His hands were everywhere as they moved together toward his bedroom. He pulled her robe back over her shoulders and let it drop to the floor. At the same time, she unbuttoned his shirt, revealing a fine dusting of dark hair.

She ached with want and need and when his fingertips brushed the sensitive underside of her breast in just a whisper of a touch, she gasped, then held her breath as he cupped first one breast then the other, teasing her with his fingertips.

He found her mouth again, kissing her longer and harder than before, revealing his own deep need.

"Rachel," he murmured, his voice husky, "are you okay with this?"

"Yes. Oh, absolutely yes."

The instant she'd kissed him back was pretty much the end of coming to his senses. But he had to ask. He didn't want her to regret it. Didn't want her to feel he'd forced her or taken advantage. He didn't want her to have expectations.

Even so, he knew he was about to cross a line. Yet he wanted this, had wanted it from the moment he'd carved her initials into the wishing tree.

He placed his shaking hands at her narrow waist, drawing her closer, then moved lower to the sweet curve of her bottom until she pressed against him. She curled a leg around his at the knee and pressed harder, providing a friction that sent him to the moon.

He eased his hand around her thigh, dipping between her legs. She was slippery and as ready for him as he was for her.

Rachel felt a wall between them disappear as she gave in to the raw, primal need.

In that sweet, sweet moment, she allowed Jake to take possession of the one thing she'd always held as her own. Her self-control.

She heard her heart pounding as hard as the rain outside, desire building and building until she reached an explosive release. She moaned, savoring the pure physical pleasure.

Jake didn't move, but held his hand against her until the spasm dissipated.

Her embarrassment lasted only until his lips met hers in a gentle kiss that took her away again, and she knew she wanted even more. She wanted everything, wanted him in every way.

She wanted the pleasure of watching him surrender in the same way she had. He must've known because his breathing became more rapid, his urgency evident as he stripped off his shorts. She pulled her nightshirt over her head.

She saw the admiration in his eyes.

She reached out to touch him, surprised at the silkiness of his skin. He groaned and closed his eyes.

She felt like a young woman who'd never experienced sex before, not a woman who'd been married for six years. And the truth was, she never *had* experienced anything like this before. Ever.

"Rachel," Jake said huskily. He reached out and pulled her down on the soft suede comforter, then holding his weight on one elbow, gently spread her legs and touched her again.

In an instant he had her at the brink, but instead of giving her release, he positioned himself over her. She was sure she'd explode the minute he entered her.

"Please," she whispered, shifting her hips.

He moved quickly to put on a condom, then in one swift motion he was there, all the way. She tightened her arms around his neck. He waited, then after a second, he stroked slowly. Hearing his sharp intake of breath, she shattered again.

She clung to everything she was feeling, even as he lowered his forehead against hers. She'd never known she possessed the ability to give such pleasure.

"You okay?" he said huskily.

"I'm better than okay," she whispered. She felt nothing less than wonderful.

"Me, too."

But no matter how she intellectualized it, she couldn't deny it meant more to her than just feeling wonderful—and she wanted it to mean more than that to him, too.

She exhaled, suddenly aware of his weight. She shifted underneath him.

"Sorry," he said. He slowly pulled away and rolled to the side, where he rested on one elbow, his other arm still across her chest.

"You were great," he said finally.

"No, *we* were great."

He looked as if he might say something else, but he didn't.

## CHAPTER THIRTEEN

IT WAS STILL DARK when Jake woke up. Alone. After they'd made love, Rachel had to go upstairs to tend to Zoe, leaving Jake to toss and turn all night, not because he wanted her again—though he did—but he just wanted to hold her and never let go.

But he had no intention of staying in River Bluff. Rachel planned to make a home here for herself and Zoe. She'd all but told him she wanted the house with a white picket fence and a bunch of kids in the yard. And she deserved to have it.

So how did he tell her "I want you, but I don't want what you want"? He couldn't.

He should leave right now, before he made things worse. Forget the bar.

Forget Rachel. It had been a week and a half since he'd applied for the building permit and a liquor license, and he hadn't heard anything, anyway.

His gut knotted. He had to finish what he started, see the Wild Card the way it should be. The way his mother envisioned it. He wasn't going to run away again. But he couldn't let Rachel believe he was staying for good, either.

He heard footsteps upstairs. Rachel was up. He had to talk to her, make sure she knew his plans. Be honest.

He heard the crunch of gravel outside, as a car pulled into the drive. That would be Cole, or one of his employees.

He tossed off his quilt and headed for the shower, but before he got there, he heard someone banging on his door. What the hell…?

"Hold your horses." He went to the door in his shorts. Annoyed, he swung open the door.

Wade Barstow stood squarely in front of him, face grim…poised for battle.

Jake's annoyance turned to anger. Mustering as much self-restraint as he could, he said lazily, "Something I can do for you?"

Barstow shifted his stance, hiked his shoulders up like a linebacker ready to charge. "You're damned right. I want you to lay off my kid."

Standing closer to the man than he'd ever been, Jake held the door with one hand and placed the other on the frame, searching Wade's face for any hint that they were related. He saw nothing—only gray eyes filled with anger…or maybe it was frustration. "Are you talking about Wyatt?"

"You know damned well who I'm talking about."

Jake bit back a retort. "I gave him a job," he said calmly. "Last time I heard, work was an honorable pastime."

"Work doesn't include filling him with ideas about quitting school and taking off on a motorcycle to see the world. Ideas that will ruin his promising future."

"If I knew what the hell you're talking about I might have an answer for you. Whatever ideas your kid has, he didn't get them from me."

"I want you to fire him."

The man had supreme gall. "He came to me looking for work. I needed someone. He's doing a good job. I think he likes it."

"It's not up for debate," Barstow said as he turned to leave. "Fire him."

Jake dug his fingers into the door, trying to keep from going after the guy. "You want me to fire him so I'm the bad guy? This kind of intimidation may work with the locals, but it doesn't work with me. I make my own decisions about who to hire and fire."

Barstow wheeled around, came back and, standing toe to toe with Jake, said evenly, "I could've had you arrested after you set fire to my barn, but I didn't out of respect for your mother. I'm asking you to return the favor."

"If I'd been the one who torched your

place, that might mean something to me. All you did was put the blame on me and let the real barn-burner off the hook."

"There was a witness."

And he was sleeping with her.

"The witness," Jake said through gritted teeth, "was wrong."

Barstow shoved a hand through his hair. "Tell you what. I've heard some talk that here in the bible belt it's tough getting a liquor license these days. You do this for me and I might be able to do something to speed things up."

Jake's blood pressure soared. "Like I said, I make my own decisions. I don't need your help. Never have."

Barstow frowned. Then his eyes narrowed as if he realized what Jake meant. He chewed on his bottom lip and for a moment, looked as if he might respond, but abruptly, he turned and walked away.

Jake closed the door, but couldn't move.

"Something wrong?" Rachel's voice came from behind him.

He stood there, his chest heaving. Dammit. As much as he tried to put the past to rest, he couldn't. The fact that he got angry told him he hadn't resolved anything. "Nothing I want to talk about." He started to walk away.

"I think you should."

He rounded on her. "Excuse me? If I don't want to talk about it, I won't."

Chin up, she looked at him. "Fine. But that's not going to make it go away. Have you ever wondered why Wyatt is working here?"

He blinked. "What do you mean?"

"His dad has money. He doesn't need a job."

"I know that. I didn't know who he was at first, and as long as he does his job, I don't care."

She went over to the sink and rinsed out Zoe's cup, poured some juice into it and gave it to Zoe, helping her hold it. "You can tell yourself that all you want."

"And what do you think the kid wants?"

She cleared her throat as she set Zoe in her seat. "He heard the rumors and came here to see you. Get to know you."

They'd never discussed the old rumors, but obviously Rachel had to have heard them, too. "Then he's come to the wrong person. He needs to talk to his father."

"And what if he can't? How could he ask his father without it sounding like an accusation? And if he thinks it's true, then he'd want to meet you. Surely you can understand that."

"Understand? No. It's a rumor. *That* I understand. My mother told me it wasn't true. That my father split before I was born. Am I supposed to believe town rumors over my mother?" He shook his head. "It's not my problem, and it sure isn't yours, so let's just drop it."

Rachel felt the sting of his words. But he was right. It wasn't any of her business, so why should she care? She brushed the hair out of her face. It didn't matter why, the fact was she did. She cared a lot. But after they'd made love, she knew what she had to do. She should've done it years ago. She couldn't let Jake go on taking the blame for something he didn't do.

Even if Jake never spoke to her again.

"I'm taking Zoe to get some things in San Antonio. If you want to go over the plans, we'll have to do it later."

Only she wasn't going to San Antonio. She was going to see her mother to call off her so-called community watchdogs. And the only way to do that was to tell her mother the truth. Jake deserved to know, but telling him now could make things worse—he might throw her out before she had another place to stay. She had to think of Zoe, too.

"I have poker tonight. We may be loud."

"It's not a problem."

In one fell swoop the tension she'd thought had disappeared returned full force.

The ride to her mother's felt inter-
minably long, but less than an hour later,
she pulled into her mother's driveway.
After getting Zoe and her tote bag
together, she went to the door, rang the
bell and waited. After a moment, she
saw the curtains move and, seconds
later, the door opened.

"I thought you might come to your
senses," her mother said.

"I didn't come here to grovel," Rachel
said, coming in and sitting on the couch,
propping Zoe up next to her with
pillows. "I came to tell you some things
and I want you to listen."

Sarah's chin went up. "You're talking
to your mother, young lady. Show some
respect."

Rachel had none to show. "But first I
want some reassurances."

Her mother frowned. "I don't know
what you mean."

"When you came out to Jake's you
said I could stay here with Zoe."

"I wanted you to stop working for him."

"Then how would I pay my bills?"

Sarah placed her fingers over her lips. "I'll give you money, if everything works out as it should."

"And if you call off your group, I'll continue to keep a secret I know to myself. If not, I'll tell everyone in town and I don't think you'll like that."

"Wh-wh-at on earth are you talking about?"

"Fifteen years ago—the night of the fire. I lied. I said I saw Jake at the Barstow stables but I didn't."

Sarah blinked. "I don't understand."

"I lied to keep you and Daddy from finding out I'd been with Kyle all night. Kyle started the fire."

Her mother didn't say anything for the longest time. Finally she said, "Kyle would never do that to his father."

"Really. And how would you know? You don't even know where I was that night."

Her mother huffed. "Well, I guess that doesn't matter now, does it? I couldn't be any more disappointed than I am already."

"What do you mean!" Rachel stood, aghast. "Of course it matters." Tears welled in Rachel's eyes, not because of her mother but because what she'd done had been horrible. Jake had suffered so much because of her.

"Mother," Rachel said, tears beginning to stream down her cheeks, "I didn't come here to apologize. I came here to ask you to stop trying to keep Jake from reopening the Wild Card."

"I'm not…it's not just me on that petition, Rachel. If you go around telling people this ridiculous story, they're just going to think you're trying to help Jake because you're sleeping with him."

Rachel squinted. "What did you say?"

"Everyone is talking about it. Everyone knows you're getting rent for services rendered."

Zoe made a noise and Rachel leaned down to keep her from rolling off the couch. She couldn't believe what her mother had just said.

"The best thing you can do is move back here and forget about that place. Jake will leave and everything will be back to normal."

Rachel's heart sank. No. Nothing would be normal ever again. She'd wanted to do the right thing and even that wasn't enough.

She gathered Zoe in her arms, picked up her diaper bag and left.

As she reached the van, she realized the worst part was that her mother might be right. Living above the Wild Card, it would be easy for people to think she was sleeping with Jake. And since Kyle had moved away years ago, she would be accusing someone who wasn't there to dispute the allegation.

She was screwed. Jake was screwed.

After placing Zoe in her seat, she started the van and headed for...she didn't know where.

She just didn't know what she could

do about any of it. Talk to the mayor? Then it came to her. Get Wade Barstow on her side, everyone else would follow.

But how the hell would she do that? Not by telling him that his oldest son had been a pyromaniac. That he'd lit the fire because he was mad at his dad. That he'd blackmailed Rachel to lie. Besides, Barstow wanted to buy the Wild Card, not make it easier for Jake to get it up and running.

Rachel stopped at the Longhorn Café. She needed to talk to someone rational. As she walked inside, she saw Stefi Martin sitting with Sally. She waved at them, then brought one of the highchairs over to a booth, put Zoe in it, sat.

A young waitress wearing the name tag Jenny came over. "Hi, there. What would you like today?"

"Coffee, please."

"That's it?"

Rachel nodded. She got out a bag of Cheerios and put some on the tray for Zoe. Shortly after, Sally left and Stefi came over and slipped into the seat across from her.

"I hear you're working for Jake now. Living there, too." She gave her a toothy smile that inferred something more.

Rachel felt her cheeks warm. "Hi, Stefi. Yes, Jake was kind enough to give me a job. And I'm renting the upstairs, not living with him."

"Well, that's a gig I'd like to have either way."

"Do you know anything of a petition circulating about the Wild Card?"

"I know there's a town meeting where they take up issues like changes that will affect the community. It's not something I go to, so I never bother to find out what's on the agenda. Why?"

"No reason."

Stefi laughed. "Well, if there's something like that, it's not likely anyone would approach me. I'd go the other way and sign a petition to open more bars just like it."

When Rachel finished her coffee, she

drove to Becky's home and had the same conversation, then hoped to hell Jake didn't find out what she was doing. Or her mother.

"So, HOW ARE renovations going?" Blake asked toward the end of the poker game.

It was midnight and Jake hoped they weren't making too much noise and keeping Zoe awake upstairs. "Great, but we're going to be stymied in a few days if that building permit doesn't come through."

"What's the holdup?" Luke asked, shoving two hundred dollars' worth of chips into the middle for the big blind. Then, after the deal, he leaned back to look at his hole cards.

"I don't know. I wish I did."

"I can check into it for you, if you'd like," Blake said.

"Sure. I could use all the help I can get. We need to get moving on this place, especially since Cole is leaving at the end of the month to bring Tessa back."

"All right, boy," Harry said slapping Cole on the back. "You sure know how to pick 'em."

"I do," Cole said proudly, then mucked his cards. "I just wish I was as lucky at poker. These cards suck." He tipped his chair back, balancing precariously on two legs.

Ed shrugged, then mucked his cards, too, leaving Jake, Luke, Blake and Harry still in the game. There were only five guys playing tonight because of some shindig in San Antonio.

"I hear there's a couple of companies trying to buy property for tract housing near here," Ed Falconetti said.

Jake set his river stone on top of his card, using it as a card holder. "Tract housing would destroy the personality of this town."

Five pairs of eyes turned toward him. "What?" he asked. "It would. River Bluff is what it is because it's small. Each store is unique. It's *Cheers* without the bar. But with the Wild Card up and running, it'll have that, too."

"You ought to run for office," Blake joked.

"Not a chance." Jake laughed, realizing he'd just defended the very town he'd spent his life bad-mouthing. Maybe he wasn't staying in River Bluff just to spite a few people.

He knew the land alone would appreciate in value if he held on to it a few years. And if he hired a general manager to keep the place running, it would be positive cash flow. Both good investments.

"There should be lots of interest in keeping the zoning as is," Jake said, thinking of the conversation he'd heard at the party between Marshall Carrick and Wade Barstow. He figured Barstow was just blowing smoke when he'd threatened him earlier about the license. "There's no other place like it within thirty miles."

"Your bet, Jake," Cole said. "You going for broke?"

"You bet your ass I am."

## CHAPTER FOURTEEN

THE WEEK PASSED QUICKLY, and Rachel couldn't believe how smoothly things were going. She'd opened a business checking and Visa account with the money Jake had given her for the project, making it easier for her to purchase what she needed. He'd also given her an advance on her salary and she'd found a sitter, Lisel Hougestradt, a retired woman who'd recently lost her husband, to watch Zoe upstairs while she worked with the small crew Cole had gathered.

She hoped Jake felt as good about how smoothly things were going. But she knew he was worried about the building permit and liquor license, especially after Blake had said he couldn't get a straight answer from anyone. Finally Jake had gone to San Antonio this morning to see what information he could get from the Office of Development Services, and when he hadn't returned by noon, she started to get worried.

"What do you think could be the holdup?" she asked Cole when he came in to use the bathroom.

"I wish I knew," he answered. "But Tessa's going to be ready soon and I'm going to have to take off for a couple of days. We have to get going on this place."

"I'm looking forward to meeting Tessa." She grabbed a bottle of water from the fridge. "You'll be the first of the Wild Bunch to get married, won't you?"

"Married again," he corrected. "And Blake is married, too."

"And what about Brady?" she asked. On poker night, she'd heard Jake and the guys teasing him about being so focused on buying a racehorse to train that he wasn't ever going to find a woman.

"Who knows?" Cole turned to Rachel with a teasing glint in his eyes. "Maybe Jake will be next?"

She felt a jolt to the solar plexus. *Jake.* "Does he—" she sputtered, suddenly unable to think. "I—I didn't know he— was seeing someone."

Cole arched an eyebrow. "I think he is, but it's hard to tell with Jake. He doesn't say too much about those things."

*Oh, my.* Did he mean her? Did he think she and Jake were… What an idiot she was. Of course he did. According to her mother, the whole town thought it. But they weren't. One night together didn't mean anything. Jake acted as if it had never happened.

"I didn't know Jake took his Harley," she said to change the subject.

"He didn't."

"But, it's gone."

"It can't be gone." Cole walked outside and went over to where the bike had been, then started toward the pecan grove.

Rachel wanted to follow, but couldn't leave Zoe by herself. A few moments later, Cole came back.

"The tracks lead out to the road. Either Jake let someone use it, or it's been stolen."

Rachel scoffed. "Who would do that here? Everyone knows Jake's bike."

Cole shrugged. "Someone passing through. Or someone pretty stupid. I guess we can't know until Jake returns."

By the time Jake came home, Cole was cleaning up to leave.

"Whoa," Jake said opening the door and seeing them right there. He took off his jacket and hung it up. "Good news. Apparently the delay was because of a rezoning meeting." He looked at Cole. "Apparently my property was under consideration for rezoning along with the rest of the acreage along the river and on the other side of the road in back that some company wanted for tract housing."

Rachel looked from Cole to Jake. "And?"

"And it's no longer an issue." He pulled a packet of legal-looking papers from a folder. "The permit and the license. I don't know what happened, but it's no longer an issue."

Jake shoved a chair out of the way, then went to his bedroom. When he came out, she and Cole were still waiting.

"So, we can go ahead then," Cole said, looking at Rachel.

"Right. Full steam."

It seemed strange. All her worrying for nothing.

Cole gave her a nudge in the ribs. "You going to tell him, or should I?"

Rachel gestured that he should go ahead.

"Your bike's gone," Cole said, just like that.

Jake frowned. "Gone? How is it gone?"

"It's not here."

Jake stormed outside. "What the hell?"

Rachel watched out the window as he searched the grounds, then followed the same tire tracks that Cole had. A few minutes later, he came back, eyes full of fire. "If I catch who did this—"

"It sucks," Cole said. "But it was there when you left. Right?"

"Of course it was."

"Well, then you've got to notify Sheriff Anderson, so he can get on it."

Jake picked up the phone and Cole went back to work. It took two minutes for Jake to give the information. Rachel heard Zoe waking up, and started upstairs.

Jake caught her by the arm. "Wait a second, will you?" He went back into the bedroom and came out again. "This is for Zoe."

"A present?"

"It's just a stuffed bear."

"You bought it for her?"

He shrugged. "I was just walking by and saw it. No big deal."

She stared at the bear, fingering the arms and legs, holding her emotions in check. Finally she looked up and said softly, "Why don't you give it to her?"

He scratched his head. "Uh, I've got to get to work. I hope she likes it," he said, then hurried off.

After Jake left, Rachel stood there, tears welling in her eyes. She pressed the soft little bear to her chest. She loved Jake.

JAKE PULLED INTO the Wild Card. He'd been driving down every street and road in and around River Bluff for three hours. He'd stopped and talked to a couple of people, but no one had seen anyone on a Harley that day.

Rachel had left before he did, saying she had some things to do in San Antonio, but he figured she should be back by now. It wasn't out of the realm of possibility that her van had broken down along some road, but given that he'd been everywhere within ten miles of River Bluff, he doubted that was the case. And she would've called someone if it was.

As he decided she was probably with a girlfriend or something, it occurred to him that she could just as easily be with a guy. The thought made him even more agitated.

He parked the truck and though it was dark, he thought he saw something move about twenty feet in front of him.

He grabbed a flashlight and went toward the movement, near where he usually parked the bike...which was there. Parked almost as it was before. The creosote bushes beyond it moved again. Without thinking he charged into the thicket, scratching his cheek in the process. He saw a dark male form curled up on the ground a few feet away, hands covering his head.

He shined the flashlight on the guy, surprised when Wyatt looked up at him. "What the... What's going on, Wyatt?"

The teen shook, but Jake didn't think

it was because he was fearful. His eyes were bloodshot. "You stole my bike."

"I'm sorry. I just wanted to ride it. I didn't hurt it or anything."

The bike was the least of Jake's worries. The kid didn't look good. "Get the hell up and come out of there," Jake ordered.

"You can't tell my dad. Please don't tell my dad."

"You steal my bike and then cry about me contacting your dad. What the hell is wrong with you?"

He had little patience with a thief. His place in San Diego had been burglarized twice. "You broke the law," he continued. "I called the sheriff. I don't think you have to worry about me telling your father. The sheriff or a judge will do it."

His bike was okay. But he'd trusted the kid, dammit. And Wyatt repaid him by stealing his property. "What else did you steal?" Jake asked.

"Nothing, I didn't steal anything."

As the young man crawled out of the

thicket, Jake grabbed his arm and jerked him to his feet. "And what made you think you could steal from me?"

On a closer look, Jake realized that while Wyatt might be high, he also looked sick. Or maybe he was just coming down.

Still holding the boy's arm, Jake tightened his grip. He wanted to shake the kid, make him realize how stupid he was.

"You're my brother, aren't you?"

The word *brother* stopped Jake cold. "Who told you that?"

Wyatt jutted his chin. "Everyone knows it."

Breathing hard, Jake said through his teeth, "Everyone doesn't know squat."

Despite doing his share of stupid things when he was a teen, Jake hadn't done half of what the people in town thought…and he'd never taken an illegal drug in his life.

But whatever he did or didn't do, it always came back to him. He loosened his grip and stepped back.

Wyatt brushed the dirt off his clothes, then straightened, his expression a mixture of defiance and confusion. "Then—then how come everyone says it?"

Oh, man. Jake realized the sixteen-year-old was hurting…but this was not the time to get into a discussion about his dubious DNA. It was not the time for empathy.

His throat dry, he swallowed. "People say it because they want answers. But that doesn't mean it's true." He rounded on the teen. "And it sure as hell doesn't give you the right to steal from me. Do you have any idea of the trouble you're in?" Did he have any idea that doing things to get even could ruin his future?

"It doesn't matter. My dad's sending me away, anyway."

But it did matter. What Wyatt did now would set him on a course for the rest of his life.

Headlights suddenly appeared on the road.

As the lights came closer and closer, Wyatt panicked. "I gotta go. I gotta go."

Jake had a decision to make. But before he had a chance, a white squad car pulled up, catching both of them in the headlights. The door opened, Sheriff Anderson stepped out and sauntered toward them, his mouth working his trademark gum.

"Oh, no," Wyatt whispered. "My dad's going to kill me."

"You should've thought of that earlier."

"Jake," Sheriff Anderson said. "Wyatt?"

"Evening, Sheriff," Jake replied. Wyatt didn't so much as nod.

"I got a call about a stolen motorcycle." He glanced at Jake's bike. "What's going on?"

Wyatt's eyes got bigger and bigger. The kid didn't look good. Maybe he'd learned his lesson. Maybe he needed a lesson. A juvenile record didn't help any kid.

*You're my brother.*

"Guess it was a misunderstanding,

Sheriff," Jake said. "I must've forgotten I'd told a buddy he could use it."

The sheriff squinted at Wyatt. "That so?"

"Yeah," Jake said. "Stupid of me, but—"

The words hadn't left Jake's lips when suddenly Wyatt keeled over, hitting the ground with a thud at Jake's feet. Both men bent over him. Jake felt the teen's forehead. "He's burning up. He needs a doctor."

Within twenty minutes, they were at the clinic and Jake and the sheriff helped Becky Howard, the only staff available, get the boy onto a gurney. Seconds later, Wade Barstow barreled inside. "Where's my boy?"

Becky was tending to Wyatt, so that left Jake and the sheriff to deal with Barstow. Jake figured he was out of it and started to walk away.

"Ask him," Sheriff Anderson said, indicating Jake.

"Chandler?" the older man said.

Barstow had told Jake to fire Wyatt. Now he wished he had. Maybe none of this would've happened.

"What the hell is going on?" Barstow asked.

Jake took a deep breath. "Becky said he needs some tests, but she doesn't think it's anything serious."

The man who might be Jake's father shoved his hands in his pockets, his expression grim. If Wade Barstow had any feelings, he sure didn't show it. "That doesn't explain what you and the sheriff are doing here."

"Your son is sick and he needs you. That's all I know," Jake said, then walked out the door.

"Jake? Is that you?" It was late, eleven o'clock, when Rachel heard a motorcycle engine. She hurried down the stairs, anxious to hear what had happened. He'd obviously found his bike.

She turned the lights on and waited. When he walked through the door, he looked as if he'd been through a war. "You look terrible. What happened?"

He hung up his leather jacket and went to the fridge.

"I heard you drive up. I guess you found the motorcycle," she probed.

He popped the top on a beer and took a swig. "Yep. And you wouldn't believe who had it."

She walked over, got out a beer for herself and opened it, waiting.

"Wyatt."

"Wyatt? Why on earth would he do that?"

He sat at the table. "Don't ask me. But the kicker is that he got sick, and Sheriff Anderson and I ended up taking him to the clinic."

"Is he okay?" Rachel sat next to him.

"Becky said he would be, so I left."

"I suppose the sheriff or the clinic notified his dad."

Jake nodded. "Yeah. He came down right away."

"I bet he was furious."

Jake raked a hand through his hair. "I don't know what he was. I left."

"You didn't tell him about the bike?"

Jake shook his head. "I couldn't. Didn't tell the sheriff the truth, either."

"I'm not sure I would've done that." She remembered how Kyle Barstow had always felt entitled. So much so that he felt invincible, as if he could do anything he wanted. He knew how to get to people, even when it required blackmail. She hoped Wyatt wasn't like his older brother. "I might have felt he needed to learn a lesson."

Jake's somber expression told her there was more to it than just Wyatt taking the bike. "Why didn't you say anything?" she persisted.

He drew in a long breath. "Because I knew why he did it. He wanted my attention. Maybe even his father's attention. He's heard the rumors about his dad and my mother." His voice cracked. "I know how he feels."

She moistened her lips and asked hesitantly, "What did you tell him?"

He laughed bitterly. "I told him the rumors weren't true. I don't think I was very convincing."

His pain tightened the lines around his eyes, the grip he had on the bottle. She reached over, placed her hand on his. "Why would you be? You don't know yourself, do you?"

He looked at her hand on his, then placed his other hand over hers. His need wrenched her heart. Words didn't come, so she laid her cheek against the top of his hand.

After a moment he said, "I need to know."

"Yes. Yes you do."

MRS. HOUGESTRADT came early the next morning as Rachel had asked her to do. Rachel said goodbye, and on her way out, she told Jake she had something to take care of.

They'd made love last night. Jake had

needed her, and she'd needed him. More than she could ever have imagined. But maybe that was because she knew it would be the last time they'd be together.

She found her way to the Barstow Ranch easily since the Bar B property butted against Rachel's childhood home. Just driving by her old place conjured bittersweet memories, but mostly she was filled with a sense of loss. There was a void inside her she doubted could ever be filled.

Her father's death almost felt more painful now than when he'd died. It had been so unexpected, she'd had no closure.

Would that be how she felt when she couldn't be with Jake any longer? They hadn't been working together very long, and had made love only twice, but it felt so natural, so right.

Pulling into the circular drive, she was reminded of how rich Wade Barstow was. The home and property could've been the prototype for an old TV drama,

*Dallas,* and Barstow could've been the character study for J.R. Ewing.

She parked and went to the door. There was no easy way to do this. And when she was finished, she'd tell Jake.

## CHAPTER FIFTEEN

IT WAS LATE WHEN JAKE got home and Rachel had fallen asleep in the chair. He didn't see her at first since all the lights were out but one yellow bulb that cast a sepia tone over the room.

Then he noticed her sitting on the couch. Surprise lit his eyes.

"Jake, I have something to say."

His expression switched to concern. "Is something wrong with Zoe?"

"No, she's fine." She indicated the chair across from her. "I went to talk to Wade Barstow today and told him about the night of the fire."

He sat forward, his expression puzzled. "You told me what happened already."

She felt parched and moistened her lips. It didn't help. She just had to get it out and be done with it.

"I only told you part of it. That night, I was with Kyle in the barn. I wasn't supposed to be there. I told my mother I was at cheerleading practice and a sleepover. Anyway, Kyle had had a fight with his father. He was furious. When I said he should apologize, he got angry with me. Then he wanted me to—to sleep with him. I refused and he said all kinds of horrible things. I tried to run away but he came after me, apologetic. I—I don't know how it happened, but I ended up staying the rest of the night." She took a breath. "I left about three o'clock in the morning. That's when I saw you."

He shook his head. "I don't understand."

She blinked back tears. "When I told Sheriff Anderson about seeing you, I never said anything about being there with Kyle or that he'd had a fight with his dad. I never told him that Kyle black-mailed me not to say anything."

Jake bolted to his feet. "Say that again."

"I didn't say that Kyle was there." She sniffled and tears started to fall. "I couldn't say anything because then my mother would know. I was so afraid someone would find out. Kyle threatened to tell everyone."

If there was one word to describe the look on Jake's face, she didn't know what it might be. Horror, disgust, disbelief?

"You let me take the blame when you knew it might've been Kyle," he said flatly. "You let me get kicked off the football team and lose my scholarship at the end of my senior year, and you were worried about what your mother would think?"

"I didn't know. I had no idea you were getting a scholarship. And then you left town and it didn't seem to matter. Six months later, Kyle left town, so no one cared what had happened."

He rubbed his face, shoved a hand through his hair. "What the hell did you think I was talking about when you came to see me that night and I told you you'd ruined my life. Did you think that was nothing?"

"Yes. I thought you were overreacting. I didn't know you'd been kicked off the team. I didn't know about the scholarship. How could I? All I can say is I'm sorry and I know that doesn't mean anything. If I had known what happened, I would've said something, no matter what."

His shoulders sagged, as if all the air had left his lungs. "That's easy to say now, isn't it? My life changed in that moment and I never had a choice in the matter. I didn't leave this town because I wanted to. I was threatened with jail. People hated me. To say you're sorry hardly makes a dent in anything."

He stood looking at her for the longest time, and she knew that anything she'd ever imagined between them was over. "I have to go upstairs," she said. "I'll be out of here tomorrow, if that's okay." As she turned to leave, she added, "Oh, for what it's worth, I also told my mother."

EARLY THE NEXT MORNING, Jake heard a car door, then the sound of a car driving away. He'd been awake all night wondering what to do.

But now, having more insight into Rachel's childhood, how could he blame her for wanting to protect herself? In her circumstances, would he have done the same thing?

There was no way to know. What he couldn't condone was that, before she started working for him, he'd asked her to tell him the truth. And she hadn't.

Did she think that making love would erase all the lies, all the hurt?

He thought about Kyle and Wyatt. Barstow knew. Would that make any difference to anyone?

On that note, he threw off his covers and went into the kitchen. A white envelope sat propped against the napkins on the kitchen table. He left it on the table and went to make coffee. Then he showered, threw on a pair of jeans and a sweatshirt.

Hearing a knock at the door, he hoped it was Rachel coming back. But it was probably Cole. He wondered how long he'd been knocking.

It was Wade Barstow.

"Can I come in?" the man asked.

Jake stepped back. He motioned for him to sit at the table. "Would you like some coffee?"

Barstow nodded. "Sure. Thanks. Black is fine."

When Jake finished, he sat at the table and waited.

"This feels very odd to me," Barstow said, looking around. "I used to come here a lot."

"I know," Jake said. Just because the guy knew the truth about the fire didn't change anything else. Didn't absolve the man for his disregard for Jake and his mother.

"I didn't come here about the fire," he said. "Though I do apologize for not looking into it more. I guess it was easy to blame you and not look at the obvious. I should have though, and I'm not proud that I didn't. But that's not why I came." He swallowed.

"I appreciate what you did last night, with Wyatt," Barstow said. "And it made me realize what I should have done years ago."

Barstow cleared his throat and went on. "I've made a lot of mistakes in my life, some I regret, some I don't. But I can't change the past."

Jake didn't know what to say. He'd wanted this conversation for so many years, but now, in comparison to his heartbreak over Rachel's revelation, it almost seemed anticlimactic.

"I loved your mother very much. I wanted to spend my life with her and—well, I didn't because she didn't want me to." He reached into his pocket and handed Jake a letter.

Jake looked at the writing on the outside of the envelope. "This is from my mother?"

"She gave it to me the last time I saw her at the hospital."

Jake didn't know he'd even been at the hospital when his mother was sick. The only person he'd seen visit was Woody, who sang at the Wild Card sometimes. He remembered how mad he'd been because out of all the people his mother had befriended at the Card, hardly anyone came to see her when she was dying.

"I was never going to show you this. But Wyatt has heard the rumors and that's why he wanted to come here, so he could see you for himself. I need to set him straight."

The rumors that Barstow was Jake's father.

"I had to show Wyatt this letter, and realize I should have shown it to you years ago. I'm sorry I didn't. But it was so personal to me."

Jake opened the envelope, took out the

letter and started reading his mother's delicate handwriting.

*My dearest Wade,*

*First, I must tell you how much I love you. If there was any other way to do this, I would, but I'm afraid I might be gone before I see you again. You've asked me to marry you so many times and though I've refused, it wasn't because I don't love you. You were married when we started seeing each other. It wasn't right, but that is my cross to bear. You are so kind, wanting to take care of Jake, but I can't let you do that. Jake is not your son. I'm sorry I misled you, but I loved you so much I didn't know what to do. You would be the most wonderful father in the world to Jake, but it wouldn't be fair to him or you to believe you're his father when it's not true. I made a mistake to get back at you, and now my beautiful boy will have to carry that burden for the rest of his life. I regret that more than anything. But I've always known we could never have had a happy life together because it would be built on the unhappiness of others. I don't believe either of us could live easily with that burden hanging over us. People make mistakes and we certainly made our share. But one mistake I made alone. I can't leave you feeling you're responsible. If you look out for Jake, I'll rest easier.*

*I will hold your love in my heart forever, and give you all my love for eternity,*
*Lola*

Jake folded the letter and put it back into the envelope. Barstow put a hand on his shoulder, then stood. "I tried to help, but you made it so difficult. Verne made it even harder...and then you disappeared." He squeezed Jake's shoulder and his voice wavered when he said, "But through it all, one thing never changed. I loved her, Jake. I still do." He turned to go. "And I would've been proud to have you as my son."

When Barstow closed the door, Jake laid his head in his arms and sobbed.

THE NEXT DAY, Rachel tiptoed into the kitchen, trying not to make any noise that would wake her mother. She didn't know how staying here was going to work out, but she'd made a deal with her mother and was going to stick by it.

The odd thing was that when Rachel had arrived, her mother had actually held Zoe while Rachel brought her things inside.

She'd have to give Jake back his key and the money he'd given her for the redesign, and she'd have to pick up the things she hadn't been able to move out of the apartment in such short notice. She'd also have to see about getting the flyers distributed.

All those things she could do. But she couldn't do anything about Jake. She couldn't stop thinking about the look in his eyes when she told him about Kyle. That was the price she had to pay for her lie. It was cheap compared to what Jake had been through.

Thinking about it now, she didn't know how she could've done such a thing. Her heart wrenched as she picked up the little bear he'd bought for Zoe. Her only consolation was that Jake would get what he wanted. People would know the truth.

The phone rang. She picked it up and looked at the number. One she didn't recognize. "Hello?"

"Rachel, it's Cole."

"Hi, Cole. What's up?"

He was quiet for a moment. "I'm trying to work here at the Wild Card, and I can't read your writing. I need you to decipher some of this plan for me."

She heard another voice in the background. Two, maybe. Male voices. "Which part are you looking at?"

"That's just it, I can't tell. It's not my forte."

"What about Jake? Can't he read it?"

"He's not here. Hey, maybe you can

come by and train me on how to read this. Then I won't need to keep calling you about it."

She thought for a moment. "How long is Jake going to be gone?"

"A while. He had to go to San Antonio."

Good. She did have things she needed to pick up as well, and maybe Cole could help her. "Zoe is sleeping right now. But if I can get Mrs. Hougestradt to sit for me, I'll be right out."

Arriving at the Wild Card a half hour later, she saw Jake's truck in the driveway. Her stomach felt queasy. Had he returned or gone to San Antonio with someone else? She got out and stood, looking around for a minute. The wind whistled through the trees and the air smelled of the river and wet red earth. She realized for the first time how attached she'd gotten to the place.

Instead of using her key, she knocked. Cole let her inside.

"Okay," she said. "What's the problem?"

"It's Jake."

"Jake? I thought this was a design problem."

"It is. There won't be any design because Jake says he's selling the place as is, and he's leaving town."

"I don't understand. Everything that happened was good. Why would he want to leave?"

"I don't know. I thought you could talk to him and he might listen."

She looked away. "I'm the last person he wants to talk to." Her voice cracked.

"Can you try?"

Pressing her lips together, she took a long breath. "Where is he?"

"Down there." He pointed. "At the river."

She placed her hands on her hips, pulse thumping. Then she saw the envelope she'd left still on the table. Unopened. "Okay."

Cole smiled. "Great."

Rachel pulled up the collar on her cable-knit sweater, then took the path to the river. There were a couple of paths leading in different directions, and she wasn't sure which one to take. She went to the right, heading for the spot where the river turned south.

As she got closer, she heard a noise in the underbrush, making her jump. "Oh, geez!" she said as a rabbit darted past her. She started laughing. "You scared me half to death, you dumb bunny."

Jake heard the female voice. He turned and saw Rachel walking toward him. His heart stilled. She looked like a nymph walking through the forest and he was reminded of his mother coming to get him so many times when he was young.

He'd made a decision to leave and yet, standing here, it was the last thing he wanted to do.

"Cole called," Rachel said. "He told me you weren't here and that he needed my help to interpret the designs."

Jake smiled. Damn Cole. Or maybe he should thank him. "He lied."

"I came to get some things, too." She tried to be easy, nonchalant. She doubted it was working.

"Are you staying at your mother's?"

Her hand went to her throat and she pulled her collar together against the wind. "Right now, anyway."

Looking at her, he wanted to take her in his arms. He'd had all night to think about what happened and he'd finally realized that no one can predict what they might do when in someone else's shoes. He kept thinking that if his mother and Barstow had loved each other so much, why couldn't they make it work? Why had his mother cheated and why hadn't Barstow been angry about it?

You can't change the past, Barstow had said. There's only today. At that moment, Jake knew that he didn't want to spend his life feeling as if he'd been denied his chance for happiness. And if he let Rachel go, that's exactly how he'd feel.

"You don't have to, you know."

She tipped her head away from the wind, holding her hair on one side so it didn't blow into her face. "Don't have to what?"

"Go. You don't have to leave the apartment."

"But Cole said you're returning to California, selling the place."

"I changed my mind."

"Just like that?"

"Just like that."

He took her hand and led her down the other path.

"Where are we going?"

"Right here." He pointed. "When I was a kid, my mother brought me out here and told me a story about a young girl whose parents beat her and called her names. But she'd come to this clearing and make wishes on this tree and if they weren't selfish wishes, they'd come true. She called it the wishing tree."

Rachel walked over to the huge tree and touched it. "If I make a wish, will it come true?"

He smiled. "I don't know. I wished a lot, but I guess they were selfish wishes."

"None ever came true?"

He thought for a moment. "Maybe more did than I realized. When my mom was dying I kept wishing she'd get better. And she didn't. Then one day I wished she wouldn't be in pain anymore. I suppose that did come true."

"What would you wish now if you could?"

"The same thing I wished when I was twelve."

She looked surprised. "What could that possibly be?"

He took her hand and brought her around the tree, then brushed off the old carving. "That."

She reached up and touched it. He saw her lips quiver. "You carved this when you were twelve?"

"I was infatuated," he said softly in her ear.

She brought her arms up around his neck, tears filling her eyes. "Twelve?"

"Twelve. I can't stop loving you, Rachel. No matter what."

"Even after what I told you?"

"But that's the past, Rachel. We have the future. Together. Here in River Bluff."

Rachel kissed him long and hard, her tears wet on his lips. Then she placed her hand on the tree and closed her eyes.

"What are you doing?"

"I'm making a wish. The same wish I made after you took me home on your motorcycle years ago."

"Can you tell me what it was?"

She smiled. "I wished you'd take me away from my mother forever."

He brought his lips to hers. "Is this far enough away?"

"It's perfect," she breathed. "As long as it's forever."

\* \* \* \* \*

*Don't miss the Wild Bunch heroes when they
deal out their* TEXAS HOLD'EM *hands next
month! (Which one will throw in his shirt
this time?) Look for Brady's story,*

Deal Me In

*by Cynthia Thomason, in February 2009
available from Mills & Boon® Superromance.*

*Turn the page for a sneak peek…*

### *Deal Me In*
### *by*
### *Cynthia Thomason*

BRADY SNAPPED THE CARDS up and re-shuffled. "I'm going to start by teaching you the basics of Texas Hold'em poker." He laid two cards in front of her and two in front of himself, all faceup. "You said you've watched the game on TV?"

"A few times."

"Good. Imagine that these two cards are the ones dealt facedown to each player at the beginning of each hand. They're called the hole cards." He flipped three more cards from the deck. "After the first round of betting, these next three are dealt. They're called the flop, and are placed in the center, faceup. Each player at the table gets to use them to make his hand. As well as—" he turned over a card "—the fourth card, called the turn." He flipped another one. "And the fifth card, known to players as the river."

Brady looked up at her, held her gaze for a moment and then cleared his throat. He pointed to the cards in front of her. "Remember, you're the only one who knows what your hole cards are. You make your first bet based on what you were dealt. And whatever you do, don't let any other player at the table guess what you might have by a change in your facial expression."

She studied Brady's face now. No wonder he was so good at this game. She could swear that the intensity of his stare had nothing to do with his enthusiasm for the game. He almost seemed to be analyzing her, not the cards. Maybe this was a strategy of some sort she didn't understand yet. If so, it was certainly effective. She crossed her legs and then uncrossed them, but couldn't get comfortable.

Two hours later Brady had knocked back both beers, but it was Molly who felt dizzy. She'd offered to get a tablet to take notes, but he'd stopped her. "No notes. This has to be second nature. If you don't get it the first time, we'll go over it again. Having it on paper isn't what counts." He pointed to the side of his head. "It's got to be in here." He stood up. "We're done for tonight."

She picked up the bottles and carried them into the kitchen. "How'd I do?" she asked when she returned and met him at the door.

"Not bad."

It wasn't the answer she had hoped for. "Spectacular" or at least "pretty well" would have been better. She went outside with him and watched him descend the steps. "Brady?"

He stopped, turned around.

"You're not angry with me any longer?"

He stared up at her for a long moment. Just before the silence became uncomfortable, he said, "You pulled a fast one and you know it. But you're here. We made a deal, and I'm not going to back out."

She went back inside and watched him out the window. "I guess I won't get any Texas-style gallantry from you," she said to herself.

\* \* \* \* \*

*Falling for the Tycoon*

*by*

*Karina Bliss*

CHRISTIAN KELLY CRIED at funerals. For a man who never wept it had been an appalling discovery. He figured the combination of somber hymns, gentle sobbing and church rituals struck some sentimental Irish chord and caused him to blubber like a baby.

He solved the problem by never attending funerals, which solidified his reputation as a hardened sinner. So it was a testament to his affection for Muriel Medina Rose that he came back to the New Zealand hometown he loathed, wearing the darkest pair of shades he could find, and stole into the last pew midway through a stirring rendition of "When the Saints Go Marching In."

Kezia Rose appreciated the irony. Knew her grandmother would have, too. Still, it started a fit of giggles she fought to control—hysteria wasn't far away. It didn't help that she stood in full view of the congregation, shaky hands clasped, waiting to do her reading.

She dug one spiky heel into the top of her other foot until tears came to her eyes. Then looked at the coffin and had to force them back. Not yet. Not until she'd done her grandmother proud.

Why hadn't she expected him?

When she felt herself under control, Kezia looked again, coolly now, to where Christian sat, a big-city cat among country pigeons. Maturity had chiseled his features back to strong bone, his thick black hair finally tamed by an expensive cut. Beneath a pair of reflective sunglasses he held his full mouth tight, almost disdainful. In thrall to a newer, stronger grief, she looked—and was not burned. A small sigh of relief escaped her.

The music faltered to a stop in that ragtag way of amateurs and the minister gave her the signal. Three steps to the podium, deep breath. She found her place in the Bible's tissue-thin pages.

Her voice cracked on the first line; she stopped. Began again, one word at a time, found a rhythm, shut out emotion. The mantle of responsibility soothed her, reminded her who she was. A pillar of the community—

teacher, chair of numerous country guilds, churchgoer. New owner of a hundred-year-old ramshackle hotel in Waterview.

The bone-dry Hauraki Plains town had sprung up around the Waterview pub, both named by Kezia's Irish forbears in a fit of whimsy and not—as Christian had once joked—to provoke a powerful thirst in the locals.

Not thinking about him right now.

The words on the page ran out; the last full stop looked like a bullet hole signaling the end of one of the happiest times of her life. Dazed, she looked up to see Christian, in classic Armani, disappear through the arched church doors. And she was glad. Glad he'd made the effort to come, gladder he'd left without making contact. She had enough to cope with today without saying goodbye to someone else she had loved.

And lost.

CHRISTIAN STUMBLED TOWARD the car park, barely able to see through his fogged sunglasses. Damn it! Temples pounding, he groped through the open window of his car for a box of tissues, yanked off the shades and mopped up the damage. Kezia's fault. The first break in her voice had brought a lump to his throat, then her words—thin, brave and clear—had sliced at his self-control like stiletto knives until he had to get out of there.

He swung around to face the gabled church and glared at its white clapboards and gray iron roof, mottled with lichen. An old-fashioned church, gravestone companions rising to the left, rose beds to the right in a riotous clash of pinks, reds and yellows. Whoever had planted the damn things had been color blind. Funny he'd never noticed that when he was growing up.

But he remembered the scent. Sweet. Lush with summer heat. He'd always been attracted to women wearing floral scents—now he knew why.

Kezia.

# Secrets always find a place to hide…

When DEA agent Rodrigo Ramirez finds undercover work at Gloryanne Barnes's nearby farm, Gloryanne's sweet innocence is too much temptation for him. Confused and bitter about love, Rodrigo's not sure if his reckless offer of marriage is just a means to completing his mission – or something more.

But as Gloryanne's bittersweet miracle and Rodrigo's double life collide, two people must decide if there's a chance for the future they both secretly desire.

## Available 6th February 2009

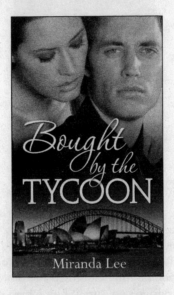

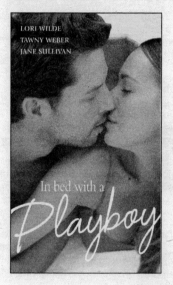

# 2 FREE

## BOOKS AND A SURPRISE GIFT!

We would like to take this opportunity to thank you for reading this Mills & Boon® book by offering you the chance to take TWO more specially selected titles from the Superromance series absolutely FREE! We're also making this offer to introduce you to the benefits of the Mills & Boon® Book Club™—

- ★ FREE home delivery
- ★ FREE gifts and competitions
- ★ FREE monthly Newsletter
- ★ Exclusive Mills & Boon Book Club offers
- ★ Books available before they're in the shops

Accepting these FREE books and gift places you under no obligation to buy, you may cancel at any time, even after receiving your free shipment. Simply complete your details below and return the entire page to the address below. You don't even need a stamp!

**YES!** Please send me 2 free Superromance books and a surprise gift. I understand that unless you hear from me, I will receive 4 superb new titles every month for just £3.69 each, postage and packing free. I am under no obligation to purchase any books and may cancel my subscription at any time. The free books and gift will be mine to keep in any case.

U9ZED

Ms/Mrs/Miss/Mr .......................................Initials ...........................................
BLOCK CAPITALS PLEASE

Surname ...........................................................................................................

Address ............................................................................................................

.........................................................................................................................

.................................................................Postcode..........................................

### Send this whole page to:
### UK: FREEPOST CN81, Croydon, CR9 3WZ